THERE'S ALWAYS A FIRST TIME...

Julie Stillwell doesn't know Sean Manning. She lives in New Jersey. He lives in New York City. But they have one big thing in common—they're both falling in love for the first time...with the wrong people.

Well, maybe not.

As director of the school play, Julie has given Roy Buckley the chance to become an actor, and he's real good at it. Good enough to become a professional. And acting's not all he's good at—now that Julie's given him the confidence to know girls find him sexy. And he says he loves Julie...but maybe not *just* Julie.

And Sara Beth Cavanaugh sure acts like she's falling for Sean. Sure they have to sneak around so nobody sees them together—since she's officially still Jack's girl. But sex means a lot to a girl, doesn't it? Sean's sure it means Sara Beth loves him and that she'll break up with Jack soon. After all, she promised.

...FOR SAYING GOOD-BYE

Other Avon Flare Books by
Bruce and Carole Hart

CROSS YOUR HEART
SOONER OR LATER
WAITING GAMES

Breaking Up Is Hard To Do

BRUCE AND CAROLE HART

AN AVON FLARE BOOK

BREAKING UP IS HARD TO DO is an original publication of Avon Books. This work has never before appeared in book form.

AVON BOOKS
A division of
The Hearst Corporation
105 Madison Avenue
New York, New York 10016

Copyright © 1987 by The Laughing Willow Company, Inc.
Published by arrangement with The Laughing Willow Company, Inc., and International Creative Management, Inc.
Library of Congress Catalog Card Number: 86-90994
ISBN: 0-380-89970-1
RL: 4.7

First Avon Flare Printing: March 1987

AVON FLARE TRADEMARK REG. U.S. PAT. OFF. AND IN OTHER COUNTRIES, MARCA REGISTRADA, HECHO EN U.S.A.

Printed in the U.S.A.

K-R 10 9 8 7 6 5 4

For Billy and Tony and Peter.
For Gracie and Ann and Sherry.
"Without a hurt the heart is hollow."

One

Looking lean and limber in a slinky black dress and heels, Julie Stillwell stood at the back of the Short Hills High School auditorium.

Up on the stage, the kids she'd cast in the Dramatic Society's production of *The Philadelphia Story* were giving the performances of their lives.

In the orchestra before her and the balcony above her, the opening night audience was rocking the rafters with peals of laughter and volleys of applause.

In all her life, Julie had never felt so happy.

At sixteen, she'd been the first girl and the first junior ever chosen to direct the Dramatic Society's annual show, and right now, the way things were going, it looked like she'd made the most of her opportunity.

The way things were going, it looked like *The Philadelphia Story* was sure to be a smash hit.

Halfway through the second act, the play was nearing its turning point—the moment when Tracy Lord, the beautiful society girl, topples from her pedestal and falls into the arms of Mike Connor, the handsome, down-to-earth reporter.

But just then, just as Tracy was teetering on the brink of toppling, Bob Patriciana barged through a door at the back of the auditorium, gasped "Thank goodness!" and brought Julie crashing back to reality.

It was Thursday morning, a few minutes before the start of school.

1

Opening night was still ten days off.

Julie was standing at the back of the empty auditorium.

She was dressed in an oversize sweatshirt and a baggy pair of jeans, under which she hoped to conceal the twelve pounds she'd put on in the three weeks since she'd agreed to direct the school play.

Bob Patriciana, her stage manager and right-hand man, was standing in front of her.

He was in a state, and it wasn't New Jersey.

"Okay," she said, bracing herself for the blow. "What is it?"

Patriciana rolled his eyes and shook his head.

"That bad?" she asked.

Patriciana nodded and said, "Steve Lewisohn."

Steve was the boy Julie had chosen to play Mike Connor, the handsome, down-to-earth reporter that Tracy Lord, the high-society girl, fell for.

"What about him?" she asked.

"He tried to call you," said Patriciana. "But you'd already gone. So he called me."

Julie told herself to be patient.

"To say what?" she asked.

"He's out."

"Out?"

"Of the play."

"No."

"He's got hepatitis."

"Are you sure?"

"He had tests."

Julie told herself not to panic.

"Is it contagious?" she asked.

"Not this kind."

"Are you sure?"

"He had *tests!*" Patriciana insisted.

Julie told herself it wasn't as bad as it might have been.

2

At least Steve hadn't given what he had to the rest of the cast.

But what good was the rest of the cast if she didn't have anyone to play Mike Connor?

"What are we going to do?" Patriciana demanded.

Normally, he was about as sweet and easygoing as a boy could be, but in a crunch he tended to get hysterical.

Calmly, as if it were no big deal, Julie said, "We're going to replace him."

"With who?"

"Whom."

"With whom?"

Julie shrugged. "Oh," she said, "with some great-looking, talented, tough-but-tender guy or other."

"Who can learn the part by a week from Saturday," Patriciana reminded her.

"Right," said Julie.

'Like whom?" asked Patriciana.

"Who," said Julie.

"Like who, then?"

Julie shrugged.

"Like Sean Penn," she said. "Or, maybe, Andrew McCarthy."

"Like who in *real life?*"

That was a tough one.

Right from the start, finding someone to play Mike Connor had been a major problem. Mike Connor was supposed to be a tough guy with the soul of a poet, a man's man that women just couldn't resist. And there just weren't a lot of guys like that walking around the halls of Short Hills High.

As a matter of fact, as far as Julie could tell, there weren't a lot of guys like that walking around anywhere.

She was only sixteen, of course, and there was always hope for the future, but so far—in all her sixteen years—

not one tough guy with the soul of a poet had crossed her path.

And it wasn't like she hadn't been looking, either. In her time, she'd checked out her fair share of tough guys, but she hadn't found the soul of a poet in any of them.

But that wasn't the point. The point wasn't whether or not such a thing as a tough guy with the soul of a poet actually existed somewhere in the Known Universe.

The point was, the guy who *played* Mike Connor didn't have to *be* Mike Connor. He just had to *look like* Mike Connor and *act like* him.

You wouldn't think that finding somebody who could do that would be such a big deal. But the way it had turned out, it was.

In fact, if it wasn't for Steve Lewisohn, finding someone to play Mike Connor might have been impossible.

Steve wasn't a tough guy, and he didn't have the soul of a poet. But he was good-looking in a slick sort of way that more than a few otherwise intelligent girls found practically irresistible. And he could act a little.

So, although she would have preferred somebody who looked a little less slick and acted with a little more conviction, with no more likely prospect in sight, Julie gave Steve the part. And, miracle of miracles, after three weeks of rehearsals and lots of hard work, it looked like he was going to work out all right.

That is, it *had* looked like that, until—

"Maybe somebody we auditioned?" Patriciana suggested.

In her mind, Julie ran over the six guys who'd competed with Steve for the role.

They were nice guys, most of them. They weren't really unattractive. Not all of them, anyway.

And they weren't entirely without talent. Most of them could read aloud.

But the truth was, as hard as she tried, Julie just

4

couldn't imagine a high-society hot-shot like Tracy Lord losing her head over any of them for even a second.

"Nobody we auditioned," she said.

Out in the corridor, the class bell rang. Julie had three minutes to get upstairs to her homeroom and into her seat. She headed for the door.

"Somebody else?" asked Patriciana, following her out the door and into the crowded corridor.

Julie nodded. "Somebody else," she said.

"Like who?" asked Patriciana.

As they reached a bend in the corridor and came to a parting of the ways, Julie stopped and turned to Patriciana.

"I'll think of somebody," she told him.

As if that answered his question, Patriciana nodded.

As he turned and bustled off toward his classroom, Julie watched after him and listened to a panicky voice shouting inside her, *Like who?*

Two

"Hey, Manning! Wait up!"

Hours later and miles away, across the Hudson River on the island of Manhattan, Sean Manning leads his troops down The Kenyon School's crowded corridor.

The captain and starting quarterback of Kenyon's football team, Sean isn't big as athletes go—five eleven, a hundred and seventy-five pounds. But he's raw-boned, lean, and hard, and there is about him—in the way he carries himself—a hint of the fires that burn inside him.

You might say that Sean was good-looking, but that would hardly cover it.

With his sandy hair, his blue-green eyes, his warm and ready smile, you'd notice him in any crowd.

But when you add to these the careless way he shakes his sandy hair into place, the way his blue-green eyes look right at you, and the suggestion of danger that dances at the edge of his smile, you've added the little things that make the difference between a good-looking guy and a heartbreaker.

Sean Manning is a heartbreaker.

You can see that by the way the girls steal looks at him as he makes his way down The Kenyon School's crowded corridor.

It's two-thirty, Thursday afternoon, and the halls are packed with kids celebrating the end of another school day.

With his wiry little placekicker, Manny Escabedo, on his left and his mountainous center, Archie Webber, on his right, and a pack of their accomplices trailing behind him, Sean is leading the nucleus of Kenyon's football team to the locker room, on their way to the football field and their daily round of practice.

"Who's gonna beat us?" Archie Webber wants to know. He answers his own question. "Nobody."

"What about Hoover?" somebody shouts from behind him.

"Punks," says Escabedo.

Sean laughs. *"Big* punks," he says. *"Fast* punks. *Mean* punks."

"Faggots," says Archie Webber.

"Sean?"

Mimi Driscoll appears on Webber's left. She is a pretty, fresh-faced little girl, a dancer with a dancer's body and a thick braid of straw-colored hair that hangs to her waist.

"Hi, Mimi," says Sean.

"Looking good," says Webber.

"Can I talk to you?" asks Mimi.

"You can talk to me," Webber volunteers.

"Who'd want to talk to you?" asks Escabedo.

"Okay," says Sean. "But I've got to get to practice."

"Or the coach will spank him," says Webber.

"It'll just take a second," says Mimi.

"Go ahead," Sean tells Webber. "I'll catch up with you."

"Yeah," says Webber, looking at Mimi and shaking his head, "but will *I* ever catch up with *you?*"

"What are you, kidding?" says Escabedo.

Webber gives him a look.

Escabedo shakes his head. "Come on!" he says. "Give 'em some room, huh?"

As the gang moves off, Sean and Mimi drift over to a spot near the lockers that line the walls.

"I thought you were going to call me," says Mimi.

"I never said that," Sean reminds her.

"I know," says Mimi. "I just thought you would."

"Sorry," says Sean.

"You had a good time," says Mimi. "Didn't you?"

"Yes," says Sean. But he's not thinking about their last date, the Saturday before last. He's thinking about their first date, the Saturday before that.

He's remembering that their first date wasn't really a date, but more of a pickup, something that happened at the end of a party.

He'd been dancing with Mimi. And Mimi danced so well and looked so good as she danced, he'd fallen a little bit in love with her.

He did that, Sean. He fell a little bit in love quite a lot—with strangers he passed on the street or saw through the window of a passing bus and, sometimes, with girls he'd known for years, girls like Mimi, who he'd suddenly see in a new light.

The problem was, it never lasted long, his falling a little bit in love. Usually, no more than a couple of dates and often less. It never ripened into something deeper or longer lasting.

Sean didn't know why, exactly. It bothered him a lot. Especially the tears.

He can see them now, welling up in Mimi's eyes. He can see Mimi fighting them back, trying to keep them from spilling over and running down her cheeks. She doesn't want to be seen standing in the middle of the corridor, crying over Sean Manning.

"I think you're a really nice girl," Sean tells her.

"Too nice," Mimi guesses.

"No," says Sean.

"But?" says Mimi.

"But . . ." says Sean.

That first time, everything had been fine. They'd left the party and gone back to Mimi's apartment and danced some more and had a few laughs and kissed good night at the door and that was it.

But something had changed between the first time and the second. Maybe it was something that Mimi read into Sean's good-night kiss. Or maybe it was just that the second time was an actual date and not just a pickup. But whatever it was, by their second date, Mimi was no longer the girl Sean had fallen a little bit in love with the week before.

In just a week, she'd transformed herself into a drowning woman who spent the whole night clutching at Sean and clinging to him, like he was the only lifeguard in sight.

The strange thing was, as close as she stuck to him and as tightly as she held on to him, Mimi never noticed that Sean was sinking beneath her weight.

"The fact is," says Sean, "I haven't been calling anybody lately. I haven't been going out. Except, you know, with the guys."

Although it's the honest-to-God truth and Sean is being as sincere as he knows how to be, Mimi doesn't buy it. She thinks Sean is just being nice.

"I thought you liked me," she says.

"I do," Sean tells her. "Really. I think you're terrific. It's just that I don't—"

"I thought you *liked* me!" Mimi shouts and, bursting into tears, she turns and races off down the corridor.

Sean watches Mimi racing away. He feels like a shit. Not because he led Mimi on. He didn't. He didn't lead her on. He didn't make her any promises. And he didn't take advantage of her. Not the slightest.

So why does he feel like such a shit? Why does he *always* end up feeling like such a shit?

As he turns and moves down the hallway, hurrying to catch up with his teammates—who by now have probably changed out of their civvies and suited up for practice—

9

Sean tells himself, No more. It's over. He's made himself a promise and he intends to stick to it.

Until he can figure out a way of avoiding these tearful endings, he's not starting anything. Until he's worked out a better way of going about it, there will be no more girls for Sean Manning. As much as he likes girls and enjoys their company, they're just too complicated, too anxious to get involved, too easily hurt, too—

At that moment, as if he needed further convincing, Sean catches sight of the one exception that proves the rule—Sara Beth Cavanaugh. She's standing by her locker, talking with her friend Marcy Bates.

Sara Beth Cavanaugh. Quite simply, she is everything a man could ask for. She's not just very pretty and very smart and very nice.

She is also exactly who she pretends to be. She isn't the least bit phony. She's *real*.

And, of course, because she is all of these things, Sara Beth Cavanaugh is also "taken."

The lucky man is Jack Ramsey—the son of Representative John J. Ramsey (Dem–N.Y.), the president of last year's graduating class, the captain of last year's varsity baseball team, and one third of Kenyon's famous Ramsey-to-Manning-to-Kauff double-play combination.

It was through playing ball with Jack that Sean first got to meet Sara Beth and see what a great girl she was and what a lucky guy Jack was.

Jack's luck has held on, too. Even though he's gone off for his freshman year at the University of Michigan and left Sara Beth behind, she still belongs to him. She's still what she was when Sean first met her and what she probably always will be—"taken."

But anyway, right now, Sara Beth looks up from her conversation with Marcy Bates, looks down the hallway, sees Sean walking toward her and greets him with a smile.

It's just a friendly smile, a long-distance "Hi, there!"

But, like always, its effect on Sean is devastating. He has to clear his throat, so his voice won't catch in it when he says, "How's Jack?"

"Super," says Sara Beth. "How's Sean?"

Sean doesn't break stride. He merely slows down as he passes by.

"Truckin'," he says. "How's Sara Beth?"

Sara Beth shrugs and smiles.

"Oh," she says, "you know."

"Yeah," says Sean.

He's past her now, looking back but moving forward.

"Are we going to beat Fieldston?" Sara Beth calls to him.

Sean calls back to her, "If you'd like."

"I'd like," she says.

"Done," says Sean. "How you doin', Marcy?"

"Hi, Sean."

"Be good," he says.

Reaching the stairwell, Sean hurries down the stairs, wondering why he'd tell Sara Beth to be good.

Considering how *wonderful* she is, for Sara Beth to be merely *good*, she'd need to have an off day.

But then, he couldn't very well have told her to be *wonderful*, could he?

She'd have thought he was crazy, wouldn't she?

And just because Jack Ramsey's girl has him talking to himself, that doesn't mean he's crazy, does it?

"Hell, no!" he shouts, and vaulting down to the bottom of the stairs, he takes off, running full-out, cutting left and right, dodging an army of imaginary tacklers all the way down the corridor, until he reaches its end and crashes through the door to the locker room and disappears from sight.

Three

Julie took off, racing down the corridor. It was lunch hour, a few seconds after noon on Friday, but she wasn't racing to the cafeteria. With the kind of stuff they served in the Short Hills High School cafeteria, that was the last place in the world anybody in his right mind would ever race to.

No. What set Julie in motion was what she was racing *from*. And what she was racing from was Dwight Burgess.

She'd seen him waiting for her in the corridor outside her solid-geometry class when the lunch bell rang at the end of the fourth period. Coming out the door, she'd ducked down in the crowd and then, as soon as she hit the corridor, she'd made a dash for it.

"Julie!"

It didn't work. Dwight saw her and took off, jogging after her. When he'd overcome her getaway jump, he fell into step beside her and said, "What have you got?"

"A headache," Julie told him.

"Yeah," he said. "I heard. Have you found anybody to replace Steve yet?"

Dwight was short, slightly built, unattractive, unkempt, and humorless.

Looking over at him, Julie said, "Have you ever considered acting?"

Blushing, Dwight said, "No."

"Don't," said Julie.

Dwight shot her a look. "Have you ever thought about *photography?*" he asked her.

There it was. Julie heaved a guilty sigh. "Not recently," she confessed.

Even though she carried her camera with her at all times and was carrying it even now, with *The Philadelphia Story* scheduled to open in just nine days, she'd all but forgotten that she was the photography editor of *The Blade*.

The Blade was the school paper, and according to Dwight Burgess, its editor in chief, it was the photograph on its front page that sold it.

Without really thinking about it, in the back of her mind, Julie had been hoping that one of her three assistant editors would come up with a decent shot for the front page of this week's edition.

"So far," said Dwight, "all I've got is cheerleader tryouts."

"Tits in knits," said Julie, shaking her head.

Beside her, porno king Dwight Burgess blushed, but stuck to his guns.

"They sell papers," he said.

"So do ax murders," said Julie.

"You got one of those?" asked Dwight.

Maybe he does have a sense of humor, Julie told herself. *Maybe he could play Mike Connor,* she thought. *Maybe I ought to have my head examined,* she concluded.

"I'll get you something," she told Dwight. "Don't worry."

"We go to bed tonight," Dwight reminded her.

"You and me?" asked Julie.

"The Blade," said Dwight.

"Thank goodness," said Julie.

She knew, if *The Blade* was going to be ready for distribution, as scheduled, the first thing Monday morning, it had to be finished and formatted ("put to bed") and turned over to the printer tonight.

"I think I'm going to be sick," said Dwight.

They'd arrived at the entrance to the school cafeteria

13

and the aroma that greeted them—a subtle blend of ammonia and soured cream of potato soup—was enough to induce anorexia.

"I wish I could join you," said Julie, "but I've got to keep up my strength."

"And I've got to keep up my circulation," said Dwight. "And believe me," he continued, "when it comes to stimulating circulation, you've got to go some to beat Bouncing Barbara Bowers."

Before Julie could shout "Pig!" Dwight turned and stalked off down the corridor.

Calling after him, Julie shouted, "I'll get you something."

But Dwight didn't turn around, and as Julie marched toward the entrance of the cafeteria, she hadn't the slightest idea what she might get him and where she'd find the time to get it.

Maybe, she thought, *if I can't come up with somebody to play Mike Connor, I can get Dwight a front-page shot of me, jumping off the roof and splatter-painting the parking lot.*

On which appetizing note, she entered the cafeteria.

Patriciana spotted her the moment she came through the door. He waved to her from a table near the windows, where he was sitting with most of the cast of *The Philadelphia Story.*

Normally, Julie would have joined them, but today being anything but normal, she thought better of it. She knew somebody was bound to ask her about Steve Lewisohn and whether she'd come up with a replacement for him yet.

She didn't want to lie to everybody and tell them she had. She hated lying even more than she hated being lied to, which she hated a lot.

But on the other hand, she didn't want to tell everybody the truth, either. She was afraid, if she admitted that she

14

hadn't yet come up with anybody to play Mike Connor, everybody would panic. And she knew that panic—a close relative of stage fright—was the last thing in the world any of them needed.

So, instead of joining the cast and sharing her problem with them, Julie returned Patriciana's wave with a jaunty little wave of her own, scrunched up her face in what she hoped would pass for a reassuring smile, and joined her friend Eleanor Davies and her usual crowd at their table by the door.

As Julie slid into the chair opposite Eleanor, Eleanor said, "Did you get anybody yet?"

So much for running away from your problems, thought Julie.

"I hear they're gonna have to cancel the show," said Lana Gaines.

"No way," said Julie.

"Then you got somebody?" asked Tiffany Scott.

"More or less," Julie lied.

Then, before anybody could ask her who she'd gotten, she looked over at the food on Eleanor's tray and said, "What's the swill du jour?"

Eleanor looked down at the unappetizing mess on her plate. "The usual," she said. "Warmish meat and glue-ish gravy."

"Yum," said Nan King.

And just as Julie hoped, everybody was off to the races, bitching about the steady stream of indigestible inedibles the cafeteria spewed out every day for lunch.

Happy to be out of the spotlight, Julie turned her attention to the brown paper bag she'd brought from home and to the single, eight-ounce container of blueberry yogurt waiting for her inside it.

It wasn't much. Not nearly enough. But Julie told herself, under the weight of the circumstances (and vice versa), it would have to do. As usual when she was under pressure, she was fighting a valiant but losing battle with her weight.

She wasn't tall. Only five feet three. And she wasn't big. Except for her breasts and her buns, which had a nasty habit of expanding from "generous" to "sloppy" at the drop of a Twinkie.

When that happened, she tried to hide her expanding assets under a wardrobe of oversize sweatshirts and baggy-bottomed jeans.

But even so, she could imagine her friends clucking over the shape she was in and saying what a shame it was, because she had "such a pretty face."

As a matter of fact, she did have a pretty face—oval-shaped, with milk-white skin, as smooth as porcelain.

Her hair—which she wore short—was a glossy chestnut, with highlights of auburn where it had been touched by the summer sun.

She had an impertinent little nose and a no-nonsense chin and a sensuous mouth, whose natural expression, owing to just the hint of an overbite, was a slightly saucy grin.

But the thing people always remembered most when they thought about Julie was her eyes. Coal-black and dazzling, Julie's eyes blazed with intelligence and glowed with humor and radiated life.

They could also gaze, hungrily, at eight-ounce containers of blueberry yogurt—which was what they were doing now.

Casually, doing her best to conceal the ravenous beast that raged within her, Julie popped the top of her yogurt, poised her spoon in the air above it, and—

Out of the corner of her eye, she noticed a flurry of activity at the far end of the cafeteria.

Without thinking, she put down her yogurt, picked up her camera, rose from her chair, and began weaving her way through the crowd to the scene of the action.

What had caught Julie's eye was Roy Buckley. A gawky six-footer, with a tall kid's slouch and a lopsided smile, Buckley was the senior class's reigning oddball.

A "brain" who set the curve on every test he took, Buckley could never quite bring himself to give a straight answer to any teacher's question when he was in a classroom. He found straight answers dull and preferred coming up with answers that were more entertaining—if not to his teachers, than at least to his classmates—even if they happened to be less right.

Given this habit of his, the fact that Buckley had earned straight A's through his first three years of high school was a real tribute to his teachers' fair-mindedness and forbearance.

But when it came to pulling one of his patented pranks, Buckley didn't count on anybody's fair-mindedness or forbearance. He always worked alone and he never took credit for his escapades, and as a result he never got caught.

Like the time he patched the filters into the intercom system so that the principal, when he made the announcements at the start of the school day, sounded like a chipmunk in a coal mine.

Nobody knew for sure it was Buckley who did it.

Or the time when the principal gave in to a drug-crazy faction of the P.T.A. and invited the New Jersey State Police into the school to search everybody's locker for controlled substances.

Even the New Jersey State Police couldn't prove it was Buckley who Crazy Glued the white flag of surrender to the top of the flagpole that stood on the lawn in front of the school.

Buckley was that smart.

Just what he might be up to at the moment, Julie couldn't guess.

But he and a few of his pals—Lou Caputo, Steve

Bender, and Chris Wise—had hustled into the cafeteria toting a steamer trunk, on the side of which they'd painted the words "WOKS NEW?"

Deserting their "warmish meat and glue-ish gravy," a crowd of kids had risen from their tables and hurried to gather round. Among them was the photography editor of *The Blade*.

Her camera to her eye, Julie was snapping away, covering the players and the action from every angle.

Moving quickly, Buckley persuaded a bunch of kids to turn their table over to him.

Then, popping the steamer trunk open, he whipped out a long white tablecloth, billowed it open with a flick of his wrists, and settled it over the table.

Next, out of the trunk he produced a parade of wooden bowls, piled high with green peppers and yellow onions and snow-white bean sprouts.

Then came a carving board, bearing a king-size slab of lean red beef.

After that there were fist-size bottles of soy sauce and sesame oil, followed by stacks of paper plates and napkins and piles of plastic knives and forks.

Finally, out of the bottom of the trunk came this enormous, tapering, round-bottomed aluminum pot—a wok—that Julie recognized from the time her mother took a stab at Chinese cooking. But unlike her mother's wok, this one was electric.

At Buckley's nod, Lou Caputo plugged it in.

Then, as Julie moved in closer, Buckley swung into action—oiling up the wok; carving the beef into slivery, thin strips; slicing the peppers and onions; grabbing up fistfuls of bean sprouts; heaping everything into his sizzling wok; stirring and seasoning and serving up his mouth-watering creation—doing everything at once and all of it asfastasthat.

As soon as they saw what Buckley was up to, a cheer

went up from the crowd. People started lining up to be served.

Lou Caputo began passing a basket, soliciting contributions for the Woks Populi Fund. Steve Bender started passing out mimeographed sheets listing the nutritional benefits of Buckley's concoction. Chris Wise cued up a tape on his giant cassette player and flooded the cafeteria with soothing "Sounds from a Japanese Garden."

The whole thing was like a party—a giant, impromptu lunch party. And Julie shot it all. Right up to the time that the principal showed up with the security guards.

Apparently, somebody must have called them. The dietitian, most likely. Who probably couldn't stand the thought of anybody actually serving tasty food in her cafeteria.

But the thing was, with his uncanny sense of timing, Buckley somehow anticipated the appearance of the riot squad and, moments before their arrival, he and his accomplices had packed up all their stuff and fled the scene of the crime.

As a result, by the time the principal, Mr. Krendler, stormed into the cafeteria, there was nothing to be seen but a bunch of kids grazing over their stir-fried lunches, as peaceful and contented as a herd of cows munching on a meadow.

With no armed riot to put down, Mr. Krendler was sorely disappointed.

"Where'd you get that?" he demanded, pointing to the food on Norm Sawyer's paper plate.

Norm looked up at him, smiled, and said, "From a friend."

Everybody cheered.

Wheeling on the crowd, Mr Krendler announced, "No one is allowed to prepare and serve food in this cafeteria without my permission."

Then, turning back to Norm Sawyer, he continued,

"Nor is anyone allowed to *eat* food that's been prepared and served in this cafeteria without my permission."

Looking up at Mr. Krendler, Norm Sawyer nodded and raised a finger to his mouth and said, "You want me to put it back?"

Everybody almost died.

Especially Mr. Krendler. "No!" he bellowed. "I do not!

"And," he continued, turning back to the crowd, "I most certainly don't want to hear of anything like this ever happening in here again. Or, I warn you, there will be dire consequences. For everyone involved."

With that, accompanied by the security guards, Mr. Krendler turned on his heels and marched out of the cafeteria.

After he was gone, everybody waited a respectful five seconds before they broke out laughing and cheering and bursting into applause.

Everybody but Julie, who couldn't afford to let her hand shake while she was still covering the action for *The Blade*.

It wasn't until the class bell rang, announcing the end of lunch hour, that she finally brought her camera down from her eye and found herself smiling.

In part, she was smiling because, in the excitement, she'd managed to forget all about eating.

But, more importantly, she was smiling because she was pretty sure that, somewhere among the seventy-two shots she'd just taken, there had to be one that would bump Barbara Bowers's bouncing bosom right off *The Blade*'s front page.

And now, as she turned and headed for the door, Julie thought of a third reason why she was smiling.

Over the last few minutes, for the first time since yesterday morning when Patriciana broke the news, she hadn't thought once about finding somebody to replace Steve Lewisohn in *The Philadelphia Story*.

Suddenly, thinking back to the look on Mr. Krendler's

face when he first realized he'd arrived at the scene of the crime too late to nab the perpetrators in mid-perpetration, Julie started to laugh.

Even as she hurried out of the cafeteria and back into the jaws of her one remaining, inescapable, and seemingly insoluble problem, she continued laughing.

She had to hand it to Buckley. He had a lot of nerve. Weird as he was, she couldn't wait to get him into a dark-room and see what developed.

Four

A pushover. That's what Fieldston was supposed to be. Three games into the season, having eked out a win over Fairfield, which was almost a girls' school, their record was one-and-two. But you wouldn't have known it from the way they played that Saturday afternoon.

They'd gotten themselves up for their game with Kenyon and, right from the start, they gave Sean Manning and his teammates all they could handle and very nearly more.

On their very first play from scrimmage, they threw long, caught Kenyon's defense flat-footed, and jumped out to a seven-point lead.

Forced to play catch-up from that point on, Sean rallied his troops again and again—throwing for two touchdowns, running for another, and handing off for a fourth.

But for all his efforts, when Escabedo failed to convert on a point-after-touchdown attempt with less than a minute left to play in the fourth quarter, the Kenyon Crusaders found themselves trailing Fieldston's "pushovers," 28–27.

If, on the following kickoff, Escabedo hadn't redeemed himself by bouncing a perfect on-sides kick off the shins of a Fieldston lineman, *and if,* as a result, Sean hadn't been given one last chance to hit Richie Boynton with a perfect pass, as he stretched out and sailed across Fieldston's goal line, then Kenyon's dream of an undefeated season and a league title would have gone up in flames, right then and there.

But as it turned out, Fate was playing favorites that day.

When Sean led his troops off the field at the end of the game, the scoreboard read Kenyon 34, Fieldston 28.

At 3–0, Kenyon remained undefeated and still tied with Hoover in the race for the league title.

But now the game is over. Now, the cheering of the crowd has faded. The pats on the back and the high-fives, the horsing around in the locker room and the showers— all of that is memory.

Sean has taken his time dressing. Lingering at his locker, he's lagged behind the last of his teammates and stolen a moment to just sit by himself and be with himself. But now the moment's past.

Rising from the bench, he moves out of the locker room, down the empty corridor, up the stairs, and on to the gym—which is packed with kids, dancing and shouting over the roar and thump of the Victory Dance.

As dances go, the Victory Dance isn't much. Just a pickup band of high school rockers fumbling through cover versions of the latest hits, and a bunch of kids dancing and clowning around. But still, this is the place to be after the game. Especially if you're looking to pick up a last-minute date for the night.

Not that Sean's here to pick up a date. Not with the memory of Mimi Driscoll, bursting into tears and running off down the corridor, still fresh in his mind.

Not when he's decided it's about time he gave the girls —and himself—a break.

The truth is, Sean doesn't know why he's here. Except he hasn't got anywhere else to go but home, and he isn't ready for that.

Actually, he isn't really ready for much of anything.

He tells himself that what he's feeling is nothing but the usual after-the-ball-is-over blues, the letdown you expect to feel when you're coming down off all the intensity and excitement of a game.

But he doesn't quite believe it. Because he knows that

feeling. He feels it after every game, week after week. And this—what he's feeling now—isn't exactly that.

What he's feeling now is something else, something different, something he can't quite put a finger on or give a name to.

But still, that's what he's trying to do, to give a name to whatever it is that's weighing on his spirit, when he hears this cheerful voice behind him saying, "What do you call a guy who makes passes at other guys?"

It's April Addams's way of saying hello.

"I don't know, Johnny," says Sean. Turning around he greets April with a smile. "What *do* you call a guy who makes passes at other guys?"

With that dead-serious way she has of cracking a joke, April bats her big brown eyes just once and says, "A quarterback!"

"Ho, ho ho!" says Sean and, in that dead-serious way he has of cracking a joke, he says, "That really stinks."

"Yeah," says April. "That's why I like it."

"Yeah," says Sean. "Me, too."

April laughs.

And Sean does, too. Because he likes April. He always has. Not as a girlfriend. Although once—one rainy day, a long time ago—there was a time. But before then and since—as a person—Sean's always liked April.

Okay, maybe she *is* a little fast and a little easy. But so what? There are lots worse things to be.

And if, like she says, she'd "rather be a slave to passion than a slave to fashion"—well, Sean's got no quarrel with that, either.

But on the other hand, just because he likes April and respects her for her insistence on being exactly who she is, warts and all, that doesn't mean he's up for the party she's throwing tonight. Not that it might not be fun to celebrate today's victory with Webber and Escabedo and the rest of the guys and their girls.

But Sean's afraid, if he goes to April's party, feeling the way he does, he's a pretty good bet to wind up either incredibly drunk or incredibly hot or most probably both, before the night is through.

Standing with April at the side of the dance floor, he imagines himself, later that night, staggering around April's apartment, leering hungrily at every girl in sight. It is not what you'd call a pretty picture.

So, even though he has no plans at all, when April says "Will I see you later?" Sean tells her he's sorry, but he's got other plans.

And April smiles like she knows what kind of plans Sean has and she says, "Why don't you bring her along?"

And before Sean can explain that there *is* no her, he sees *her!*

"I'll be damned!" he says.

April follows Sean's gaze across the dance floor, where Sara Beth Cavanaugh has just walked in the door with Marcy Bates and Marcy's regular date, Gary Steinbrenner.

As far as Sean can remember, this is the first time that Sara Beth has showed up at a Victory Dance since last year, when she used to drop in with Jack Ramsey.

"I wonder what she's doing here," says April.

"Probably horny," says Archie Webber.

Laughing at his own joke, he steps up beside April and joins the party.

Only April gives Webber a look and Sean doesn't crack a smile, so Webber says, "Hey! With Jack Ramsey off at Michigan, what do you expect? I mean, she's only human, isn't she?"

"Is she?" asks April.

"I don't know," says Sean, who hasn't taken his eyes off Sara Beth since he spotted her.

"I guess you'd have to ask Jack," says Webber, laughing again. "Hey! Where you going?"

Sean's decided, as long as Sara Beth's here, he ought to

be friendly and say hello. He imagines, without Jack around, she must be feeling pretty lonely.

Although, he reminds himself as he moves across the floor to her, if ever a girl didn't need to feel lonely for one second more than she wanted to, it's Sara Beth Cavanaugh.

It's outrageous how truly beautiful Sara Beth is. On a purely objective level.

On the one hand, she's tall and leggy and as coltish as a cowgirl. But on the other hand, she's as civilized and cultured, as delicate and demure, as a drawing-room debutante.

And sometimes, like now, when Sara Beth wears her raven-black hair loose about her shoulders, so that it frames her pretty face with its finely chiseled features and its ivory-smooth skin and sets off her dazzling emerald eyes, she reminds Sean of some Legendary Heroine, sprung from the pages of an historical romance, an Untamed Beauty with a Fiery Temper and the Blood of Kings Flowing in her Veins, A Champion of the People, A Defender of the Faith, A Warrior Princess of the Ancient Emerald Isle!

"Thanks," she says, when she sees Sean approaching her.

Snapping himself out of his fantasy, Sean says, "Huh?" Then, as if he'd just noticed Sara Beth, he says, "Oh, hi." And then he says, *"Thanks?"*

Sara Beth smiles at him, as if she hasn't noticed he's acting like a total jerk.

"For beating Fieldston," she reminds him. "Remember? You said you'd beat them if I liked?"

"Oh, yeah," says Sean. "I did say that, didn't I?"

"Are you all right?"

"Sure," says Sean. "Couple of bruises. Nothing much. How are you?"

"Couple of bruises," she says, shrugging. "Nothing much."

Sean laughs and says, "You're Irish, right?"

"Cavanaugh?" she says.

"I'm sorry," he says, as he notices the band has stopped playing. "Did you want to dance?"

"Are you sure you didn't get hit in the head?" she asks him.

Sean laughs.

"No I'm not," he says. "It's cumulative, you know. They say, after a while you reach a point where your whole skull gets kind of . . ."

"Numb?"

"Yeah," says Sean. "That's it."

Sara Beth laughs. "You were terrific out there today," she says.

"Aw, shucks!" says Sean, covering his very real embarrassment with a cornball grin.

"But you know that," Sara Beth teases.

Changing the subject, Sean says, "How come you decided to . . . ?" He nods toward the dance floor.

"Marcy's idea," says Sara Beth. "She loves to dance and Gary is a klutz, so . . ."

"Oh," says Sean.

Suddenly, just looking at Sara Beth, he can't think what else to say. He's speechless.

A very long moment passes with him just standing there, staring at Sara Beth, and her just standing there, smiling at him, until—desperate to say *something*—he finds himself saying good-bye.

"Well," he says, edging toward the door, "it's nice seeing you. But I guess I'd better be going. So take care, now. And say hi to Jack next time you talk to him, okay? Okay, then. Bye."

And he's out the door and standing in the corridor and wondering what the hell he's doing there and what he ought to do now.

He can't go back inside. Not after he's just told Sara Beth he had to leave.

27

But now that he thinks of it, there's no point in his going back inside anyway.

Whatever it was he came here to do, he's probably done it by now or, if he hasn't, he's probably better off just leaving it alone.

So he heads upstairs to his locker, where he's left the book he's been reading—*The Great Gatsby* by F. Scott Fitzgerald.

It's a good book, unbelievably better than the movie, and the way the night is shaping up, it looks like a good book and a hot bath is about as good as it's going to get.

Which, when he thinks about it, isn't really all that bad.

In fact, by the time he's grabbed his book out of his locker and gotten back downstairs, he's actually feeling pretty all right about his plans for the evening.

In fact, as he walks out of the school's front door, the nameless depression he was feeling just a few minutes before is showing signs of lifting.

Or maybe it's just the lift that he gets when he sees Sara Beth standing at the curb, right in front of the school, waving good-bye to Marcy and Gary, as their taxi moves off down the street.

As Sara Beth turns to look for another taxi, Sean calls to her, "You'd probably have better luck at the corner."

Smiling, as if just the sight of Sean somehow amused her, Sara Beth says, "That's just what I was thinking."

So they walk to the corner together and, when Sara Beth decides to keep walking—because it's such a beautiful day, it's a shame to waste it sitting in the back of a taxi— Sean decides to keep walking, too.

It doesn't matter that he lives on the West Side, only a couple of blocks from school, and Sara Beth lives all the way across the park on the East Side, because Sara Beth is right, it is a beautiful day.

The air is crisp and clear, like it sometimes gets when

it's autumn in New York. Like it's blown in from somewhere high up in the mountains.

And the sun is shining with a brilliance that casts sharp-edged shadows and makes everything you set your eyes on jump out at you, radiant, more real than real, and more beautiful than you'll remember it, once the day is past.

Sean wishes he had his camera with him, his "memory maker," as his father called it when he gave it to him, just before he moved out and started turning himself into a memory.

But, hey, Sara Beth? In this light? Sara Beth playing tag with flocks of pigeons? Sara Beth kicking up clouds of autumn leaves? Sara Beth waving at the kids on the carousel? Sara Beth laughing at the antics of the seals? Sara Beth in silhouette with Windemere Castle framed against the jittery skyline, under a seamless sky? Those are images a guy wants to hold on to forever.

But here's the amazing thing, the really exceptional thing—for Sean, looking at Sara Beth, as terrific as it is, is less than half the fun of being with Sara Beth.

Once you get past how beautiful she is and get over trying to impress her with what an ace you are, Sara Beth is great company. She's really comfortable to just walk along with. And really easy to talk to.

"Party tonight?" she asks Sean.

"No, thanks," Sean answers.

Sara Beth laughs and gives him a look. "Seriously," she says.

"Yeah," says Sean, dismissing it with a shrug. "At April's. But I'm not going."

"What?" She says it like she's amazed. "Sean Manning? Passing up a party? I thought you were a party animal!"

It's an old game, one they used to play when Sean hung out with Sara Beth and Jack last year during baseball season. Sara Beth and Jack were always kidding him about all his parties and all his girls.

The way it went, Jack always pretended he was jealous of Sean, and Sara Beth pretended she felt sorry for all the girls whose hearts he was breaking. She used to say it would catch up with him.

If he didn't settle down, she'd tell him, someday when he least expected it some little girl was going to come along and break his heart.

"I've put all that behind me," says Sean.

"Uh-huh."

"No, I have," says Sean. "At least for a while. I've kind of dropped out."

Sara Beth doesn't say anything for a second, but from the smile on her face and the look in her eye, Sean can see she doesn't believe a word of what he's told her.

"So, where *are* you going tonight?"

"Home," says Sean. But then, when he realizes how pathetic that sounds, he adds, "And then out to dinner with my father."

Right away, Sean's sorry that he's lied and sorrier still that it's his father, of all people, who he's chosen to lie about. If there's anything he doesn't feel like talking about, especially now, it's his father.

But he doesn't have to worry about it because—as if she'd guessed how he feels—Sara Beth says, "Oh. That's nice." And lets it go at that.

And then, somehow, as they continue ambling through the park, the conversation swings away from Sean and around to Sara Beth.

Maybe Sara Beth swings it or maybe it just swings itself, but either way, Sean's happy to let Sara Beth carry the ball for a while.

She's a pretty good talker and what she's got to talk about—the life she leads and the life she's led—is pretty fascinating. Not to mention enviable.

Sara Beth's father, Francis X. Cavanaugh, is in the construction business. You can see his name on construction sites all over New York City. But that's not the half of it.

Francis X. Cavanaugh's name is also on construction sites all over the world, and ever since Sara Beth was old enough to travel, her father's been taking her and her mother with him to Europe and South America, Japan and the Middle East—to the best of the places where his business has taken him.

So, as a result, Sara Beth's been to all of these incredible places and met all these incredible people and seen all kinds of incredible things—which can make a person incredibly interesting, especially to a cluck like Sean, who has yet to set foot outside of the continental United States.

So, with one thing and another, although they spend the better part of an hour walking and talking, when Sean and Sara Beth finally arrive at the Cavanaugh's town house—on East End Avenue, just across the street from Gracie Mansion—it seems to Sean like they've gotten there in no time at all.

Pausing at the bottom of a steep flight of stairs that leads up to her front door, Sara Beth says, "Well, this is it."

Sean looks up at the stately, four-story brownstone, at the ivy creeping up its handsome façade to its tiled roof.

"Cute," he says.

"Be it ever so luxurious," says Sara Beth.

"Yeah," says Sean.

And then, for the first time since the dance, there's one of those awkward moments when Sean doesn't know what to say next and Sara Beth just stands there smiling at him, while the time lumbers by.

Finally, Sara Beth says, "It isn't true, is it? What you said? About not going out?"

Sean shrugs and says, "It's only been a couple of weeks, but, yeah."

Sara Beth looks at him, like she still isn't sure if he's just kidding or if he's really being serious.

"I mean, it isn't like a vow, or anything," Sean tells her. "It isn't supposed to go on forever, but . . ."

He pauses a moment, wondering if he should go on.

"I don't know," he says. "It always starts out being one thing and winds up being something else."

"Always?" she asks.

He nods and says, "Sooner or later."

"So you quit?" she asks.

"What's the point?" he asks.

She looks sad and sympathetic.

Another one of those long silences comes and goes.

She smiles a sad little smile and says, "I guess that kind of puts us in the same boat, doesn't it?"

"Yeah," says Sean. "I guess it does, doesn't it?"

He's never thought of it just that way.

"You think . . . ?" he says. But he stops himself. It's a crazy idea.

"What?"

"No," says Sean. "It's too dumb."

"What is?"

"Oh," he says, "I was just thinking. If Jack wouldn't mind. And you wouldn't. I mean, maybe we—you and me—maybe we could not go out together sometime."

She doesn't laugh.

She just looks at him for a second and then she says, "You mean, like, just hang out?"

"Yeah," says Sean. "Like this."

She thinks about it.

She looks down at the ground and then back up at Sean and she says, "I don't know."

"Yeah," says Sean. "It's a lame idea."

"No," says Sara Beth. "I mean, maybe it is."

"Well," says Sean. "It's no big deal."

"No," Sara Beth agrees. "I know."

"But you know," says Sean, shrugging like it's no big

32

deal, "if it's all right and you feel like it sometime, we could try it—not going out together."

Sara Beth smiles.

"I'll not think about it," she says.

"Good," says Sean. "Don't."

"I won't," she promises. "Thanks for walking me home, Sean."

"Sure," he says. "It's the best time I haven't had in a long time."

She laughs and says, "Bye."

He watches her as she turns and hurries up the stairs and lets herself in her door. Then he turns and walks away.

After he's taken a few steps, he finds himself whistling. A few steps more and he recognizes the tune.

It's the Beatles' "You say Goodbye and I say Hello."

Five

Buckley was a hero. His caper in the cafeteria did it, but the front page of *The Blade* the following Monday morning confirmed it. Thanks to ace photographer Julie Stillwell, Buckley was the star of a photo comic strip that covered *The Blade*'s front page.

In a series of nine photos—to which Julie had added little hand-lettered word balloons that streamed up out of people's mouths—the photo comic strip told the whole story of Buckley and his magic wok from beginning to end.

Well, not quite the whole story. In order to protect the guilty, in each of the photos Julie had painted a Lone Ranger mask over most of Buckley's face. And, as an added precaution, she'd made up an alias for him. She'd named him—and the comic strip—Wokman!

At the time she came up with the name, Julie thought it was pretty hot. But now that *The Blade* was out, she wasn't so sure.

What worried her was how Buckley was going to feel when everybody and his uncle started calling him by the name she'd given him.

"Hey, Wokman!"

She could hear it now, echoing down the school corridors. She hoped the clown prince of Short Hills High could take a joke as well as he could play one. Because she had plans for him.

It started in the darkroom last Friday after school, while

she was watching Buckley's features taking shape on the print sheets she'd dropped into *The Blade*'s developing solution.

She decided Buckley was cute.

Up until then, if she'd thought about Buckley at all, she'd thought of him as kind of comical looking. But when his face started swimming up at her from under the developing solution, she saw—for the first time—that he was actually rather nice looking.

His hair was a tangle of tight, silky brown curls, worn short at the top but long at the sides and back, so it fluffed out over the back of his collar.

His cheekbones were high and prominent, which gave his cheeks that hollow look you sometimes see in young Frenchmen and high-fashion models.

His jaw was strong and his mouth—with its slightly pouty lips—seemed always on the verge of an ironic smile.

But it was Buckley's eyes, his funny-sad eyes, gazing up at her through the developing solution, that finally got to Julie. She'd never looked into Buckley's eyes before.

She had the distinct impression there was somebody vulnerable and caring behind the supercool wiseguy in Buckley's eyes.

But she realized that this was much too big a conclusion to jump to on the evidence of a few photographs—even photographs that she herself had taken.

So she decided that Buckley was cute and she let it go at that.

Except she didn't let it go.

Because late Sunday night as she was lying in bed, trying not to think about Mike Connor, it suddenly came to her—as smart and funny, as nervy *and as cute* as he was, Buckley might make a perfect Mike Connor!

Okay. Not perfect. She had to admit, right off, Buckley

wasn't exactly the Mike Connor that Philip Barry had in mind when he wrote *The Philadelphia Story*.

His Mike Connor was more of a square-jawed, warm-hearted type of character that women can't help but fall madly in love with. Which Buckley certainly was not.

But on the other hand, Buckley *was* smart enough to learn his lines quickly. And funny enough to see the humor in the part he was playing. And daredevil enough to risk getting up on a stage and making a fool of himself in front of a bunch of strangers.

And if those weren't reasons enough for Julie to go after Buckley, there was the fact that opening night was only six days off and, as hard as she'd tried, she hadn't been able to think of anybody other than Buckley who might be able to act the part and might be willing to take it.

"You've *got* to be joking!" said Bob Patriciana.

She caught up with him at lunch hour. He was on his way to the cafeteria, but she'd grabbed him and hauled him into an empty classroom.

She'd decided this morning on the way to school, before she tracked Buckley down and popped the fateful question, she'd better try out her "inspiration" on someone whose opinion she respected.

"The boy's a positive loon!" said Patriciana.

From the way he said it—close up and looking her straight in the eye, in that ultra-sincere way he had—it was obvious Patriciana thought that Julie had lost her mind.

Which was possible, she had to admit. With opening night bearing down on her the way it was, it was possible that anyone at all—even *William F.* Buckley—might suddenly start looking cute and seeming like he was born to play the part of Mike Connor.

So Julie listened closely as Patriciana pointed out a few of Buckley's more obvious shortcomings.

Aside from Buckley's being a *"loon,"* Patriciana pointed out, he'd never *acted* before. Not that anyone ever *heard* of. And there *had* to be a reason for *that*. Lack of *talent*, most likely.

And *surely*, Julie didn't have to be reminded that there was a *world* of difference between *showing off* in the school cafeteria and *acting*. On a *stage*. In front of an *audience*.

And even if there *wasn't*, Patriciana insisted—*whoever* Julie chose to play the part of Mike Connor—he simply *had* to be *handsome*.

Or *charming*, at the very *least!*

And *Buckley*, in case Julie hadn't *noticed*, was conspicuously *neither!*

"There simply *has* to be somebody better around," he concluded. "*Anybody* would be better. Even *me!*"

Julie couldn't stop herself from laughing. But she couldn't stop herself from throwing her arms around Patriciana and giving him a big hug, either.

They both knew there was no way he could get away with playing a lady's man like Mike Connor. Not in this life.

But nonetheless, Julie was grateful to be reminded, especially at a time like this, as long as there were still people like Patriciana around, chivalry was not dead.

"Wish me luck?" she asked him.

"*Luck* will hardly do," he replied. "What *you're* after is a *miracle!*"

"Wish me a miracle?"

Raising his eyes skyward, Patriciana replied, "Heaven help us!"

With which benediction, Julie went awooing her "Wokman."

Six

"I make that kick—that on-sides kick—perfect. But you think that sucker says, 'Nice goin', Manny'? Or anything else about it?

"No, man. What he wants to know is how come I missed the point after.

"Was it Webber's snap? Or the way Manning held it? Or was it just me, screwin' up as usual.

"You believe it?"

Sean believes it. In fact, it's so typical of the coach, he has to smile.

"What did you tell him?" he asks.

Escabedo shrugs and says, "I told him it was you."

Sean laughs.

And so does everybody else. They're all sitting together in the school cafeteria, eating lunch at the football team's unofficial training table.

Sean shakes his head and tells Escabedo, "It wasn't me. It was Webber."

Down at the other end of the table, Webber looks up from his hero sandwich and says, "Bullshit!"

Everybody laughs.

Except Escabedo. Still looking at Sean, he shrugs and says, "Maybe. But the coach wants to see you."

Everybody laughs again.

"Did I tell you?" says Webber, showing Sean a yard-wide grin and a mouthful of hero sandwich.

"When?" asks Sean.

"Now," says Escabedo.

"Fumble-fingers!" says Webber.

Everybody laughs.

Sean, too. He takes one last spoonful of his yogurt and then, getting up from the table, he says, "He probably just wants my autograph."

Everybody groans.

"Probably trying to impress his girlfriend," he says. "She probably doesn't believe he really knows me."

Everybody groans louder, as Sean turns and makes his way out of the cafeteria and heads off toward the coach's office.

On his way, he finds himself imagining how his meeting with the coach will go. It isn't hard to imagine because it always goes the same way.

The first thing, when he walks into the coach's office, the coach won't notice him. He'll be bent over his desk, pretending he's busy with paperwork.

Then, when the coach *does* notice him, he'll act like he's surprised to see him.

Then, as if he hadn't thought about it until just then, he'll suddenly "remember" Saturday's game.

And "remembering" Saturday's game, he'll get this disgusted look on his face.

And even though he's still younger than middle-aged and stands six feet four and weighs better than 250 pounds, he'll start shaking his head and clucking his tongue like a little old lady.

And then he'll say, "Manning . . ." Like it's the name of his favorite grandson, who just got caught red-handed, passing top-secret government documents to the Commies in exchange for a thimbleful of crack.

And that's *all* he'll say.

Just "Manning . . ."

Until Sean picks up his cue and says, "Yes, coach?"

Like he doesn't know what's coming.

Which the coach will take as *his* cue to begin this week's lecture, covering everything Sean did wrong on Saturday and nothing he did right.

Which lecture the coach will eventually conclude by warning Sean, if he doesn't shape up, "Horace Mann's going to whip your ass next Saturday, and then you can kiss off that big-time college scholarship you've got your heart set on and everything that goes with it!"

Which, as it turns out, is almost exactly the way it actually goes.

"Well," says the coach, leaning back from his desk, folding his hands behind his head, and exposing a gut the size of a pregnant bear's. "What have you got to say for yourself?"

Standing there, across the desk from the coach, Sean isn't exactly sure what he'd say for himself, if he actually spoke for himself.

Deep in his heart, he isn't at all sure that a big-time college scholarship and a big-time career as a big-time college athlete is what he really wants.

He knows it's what everybody *thinks* he wants—the coach and his father and his mother and everybody else.

He knows it's what everybody *expects* him to want.

He knows it's what everybody *wants* him to want.

Because everybody wants the best for him, and being an All-American superstar with his face on the cover of *Sports Illustrated* seems to be everybody's idea of "the best."

Things would be a lot simpler for Sean if he just agreed with everybody.

But he's already spent the better part of his life being some kind of junior superstar and, more and more, especially lately, it's beginning to feel like junior superstardom —and "everything that goes with it"—isn't really all that much.

40

In fact, he's beginning to suspect that even senior super-stardom is a whole lot less than it's cracked up to be.

That's what he'd have to say for himself, if he actually spoke for himself.

But there isn't much point in doing that here or now. For here and now, saying what the coach wants to hear will do.

"I'll try to do better this week," Sean tells the coach. It's what he tells him every week. It's little enough to promise and, usually, it's enough to do the trick.

"You'd better," says the coach.

As usual.

"Right."

With a nod, Sean turns to go.

"Aren't you going to ask me why?" says the coach.

This is a new wrinkle in the script. The coach is improvising.

Turning back to him, Sean says, "Why?"

The coach doesn't answer right away. He just smiles. And then after a second he says, "Because Don Jellinek's coming down from Notre Dame to see you play, that's why."

"Oh, yeah?" says Sean.

It's the moment everybody's been waiting for. Sean's first chance to impress a big-time college-football scout.

Don Jellinek. If Sean can show him something this Saturday, he can just go right on showing him and the rest of them more of the same, week after week, for the next four years.

And, maybe, after that, if he's really good and he hasn't come up with something better to do with his life before then, he can go right on doing the same thing for another five or ten years—until the legs go or reflexes slow or some kid better than him comes along and takes his job away.

And then . . .

"Yup," says the coach, like the host of a game show,

opening the curtain on a million-dollar prize, "this Saturday, a big-time scout from a big-time school is flying in to take a look at you. What do you think of that?"

Sean half wishes he could muster a little enthusiasm for the coach's sake. But he can't.

It's all he can do to sound halfway sincere when he says, "That's great, coach. Thanks for telling me."

"And if he likes what he sees as much as I told him he would," says the coach, "he might want to talk to you after the game."

"Great," says Sean.

"Is your father going to be around after the game?"

"He usually is."

"He'd want to talk to him, too," says the coach. "If he likes what he sees. Will he?"

At this moment, the coach reminds Sean of an animal trainer, holding out a cookie to his pet spaniel, trying to get him to do a trick for it.

He tells the coach, "I'll try to do better than I did last week."

"You'd better," says the coach.

"Is that it?"

The coach nods.

"See you at practice," says Sean.

"Yeah," says the coach, as Sean turns to go. "And Sean?"

"Yeah?"

"Tell Webber I want to see him."

Sean smiles and says, "Right, coach."

And then he's history.

Seven

When Buckley showed up for his computer-sciences lab, right after lunch—and just as the bell sounded, making Julie late for her class in American history—Julie was waiting for him outside the door.

Buckley spotted her as he was coming down the corridor, and then—although he'd never spoken to Julie before, and stopping to speak to her now would make him late for his class—Buckley stopped in front of her and said, "Dr. Frankenstein, I presume."

Julie laughed.

And she blushed, too. Because she had to admit it. In her own little way, by plastering Buckley's picture all over the front page of *The Blade,* she *had* created a monster. And she *hadn't* bothered to ask the monster's permission.

"I hope you don't mind," she said.

"It could have been worse." Buckley shrugged. "I could have been Igor."

Julie laughed.

He *was* funny. And he was *cute.* And she *knew* he had nerves of steel.

But can he act? she wondered. *And will he?*

She took the plunge. "How would you like to be in a play?" she asked.

"Your play?" asked Buckley.

"Philip Barry's," Julie answered.

Buckley smiled and shook his head. "No way," he told her.

She handed him the playbook.

"Read it," she said.

He took the playbook.

Good, she thought.

He looked at the playbook, then raised his eyes and looked all around him.

"Here?" he asked.

"The auditorium," she answered.

Without another word, she turned and set off, on her way there.

Buckley called after her, "It's locked."

Without looking back or breaking stride, Julie answered, "I've got a key."

"Wait a minute!" Buckley protested.

She turned to look at him. He was walking toward her, coming to join her.

Yippee! she thought.

She wouldn't dare say it. Or even let herself smile. She still had a very long way to go.

As Buckley caught up with her, Julie told him, "We don't *have* a minute. You go *on* Saturday night."

As they moved together, through the corridors and down the stairs to the auditorium below, Buckley asked Julie about the play and his part in it.

She told him *The Philadelphia Story* was a great play. It had been delighting audiences and making stars out of actors ever since it was first produced on Broadway, almost fifty years ago.

It was a very funny romantic comedy about a rich society girl who gets saved from marrying the wrong man by a down-to-earth reporter who—on the night before her wedding—teaches her the difference between being a perfect lady and being a real woman.

Buckley's part, the part of the reporter, Mike Connor, wasn't a *long* part, she told him—he didn't get the girl— but it was a *big* part, a *pivotal* part. The fate of the play—

its success or failure—was in the hands of the actor who played it.

Buckley smiled his smile at that.

"Will it make me a star?" he asked.

Julie laughed.

"It made Van Heflin," she told him.

"Who?"

"Did you ever see *Shane?*"

"No."

"You should. It's the best. He's in it."

"Van Halen?"

"Heflin," she corrected him. "Anyway, it's a great part. You're the guy who sweeps Tracy Lord off her feet. You're the one who gets to thaw out the ice queen."

"Oh, yeah?"

He liked that, she could tell.

"She can't resist your good looks and manly charm."

Buckley laughed.

"You sure you've got the right guy?" he asked.

"I wasn't," Julie admitted. "Until I saw how much you wanted to do it."

She unlocked the door to the auditorium, opened it, and stepped inside.

As he followed Julie into the auditorium, Buckley said, "What makes you think that?"

Julie didn't answer him.

Instead, leading Buckley down the aisle, past the rows of empty seats to the dimly lit stage below, she said, "What is it? The limelight?

"Or proving how smart you are by learning the part in such a short time?

"Or maybe you're a knight in shining armor, who just can't say no to a damsel in distress?"

She led him up the steps at the side of the stage, crossed to a folding card table that was set up at the stage's front edge, and took a chair.

Motioning Buckley to take the chair opposite her, she said, "Just why *do* you want to do it?"

"I don't," said Buckley.

He sat in the chair opposite her.

"I probably won't," he said.

"Scared?" she asked.

He smiled his crooked smile.

"Sheee—"

"It's okay," she assured him. "Everybody is, the first time. It is the first time, isn't it?"

"I was in a Christmas pageant once," he told her. "In the manger scene. I played the ass."

He laughed.

It was a nice laugh, a thoroughly delighted laugh.

"That's it?" she asked.

"How about you?" he asked. "Do you know what you're doing?"

"Page seventy-six," she told him. "I'll read Tracy. You read Mike."

"Mind if I read it over first?" he asked.

"No," she said. "Go ahead."

It was the most important scene in the play, the turning point, where down-to-earth Mike and upper-crust Tracy put their class prejudices aside and melt into each other's arms.

By reading the scene with Buckley, Julie would get a chance to see how he played both sides of Mike Connor's character—his rough exterior and the deeply romantic soul it conceals and protects.

Sitting across the table from him—watching the emotions playing over his face, as he read the scene over to himself—Julie wondered what kind of soul Buckley's rough exterior was concealing and protecting.

"We kiss?" asked Buckley, nearing the end of the love scene.

"Only in the *play*," Julie assured him.

He looked *relieved!*

What soul? Julie asked herself.

To Buckley, she said, "Ready?"

He held up one finger as he breezed through to the end of the scene.

Then, finishing, he looked up at Julie, shook his head, and said, "I can't do it."

Julie asked him if he'd had a good time at the party.

Which was the way the scene between Tracy Lord and Mike Connor started.

Buckley just looked at her for a second and then he nodded and said yes, he'd been richly entertained.

Then quickly he flipped through his playbook, back to the start of the scene.

And they were off, playing the scene word for word, exactly the way Philip Barry wrote it.

Five minutes later, it was over.

A little tipsy from champagne and Mike Connor's kiss, Tracy Lord was running off with him for a midnight dip in her heated swimming pool.

And that was it.

"Sorry," said Buckley, scraping his chair back from the table.

"You were *good!*" said Julie.

He'd been better than she'd hoped. *Really* good at the rough exterior part, but—

"But you can't let yourself get embarrassed by the romantic stuff," she told him. "At least, no more embarrassed than Mike Connor would be. Which I don't think would be very much. Reporters, you know, they were like the rock stars of the thirties."

She thought he'd find the comparison flattering. And judging by the self-conscious smile that flickered over his face, he did. But, apparently, winning Buckley over was going to take more than flattery.

"Look, Doc," he said, "I appreciate being sprung from

class and everything. And this has kind of been fun and everything. But, be real!

"Me? Doing this? In front of nine gazillion people? This Saturday night?

"I'd love to help you out, Doc, but no thanks, really."

He stood up and turned to go.

"Do you know who's playing Tracy?" Julie asked him.

It was her trump card, one she'd been hoping not to play.

"It doesn't matter," said Buckley.

"Kelley Seaver," said Julie.

It mattered. She could see it.

Shit! she thought. *He's taken the bait.*

"The new girl?" asked Buckley.

Thank God! she thought.

She hated herself for dangling Kelley Seaver in front of Buckley. But she hated Buckley just as much for falling for it.

But then, she wondered, *what red-blooded, pea-brained high school boy* wouldn't *fall for Kelley Seaver?*

A transfer student in her senior year, Kelley was, without a doubt, the most beautiful girl anybody around Short Hills High School had ever seen.

In fact, it was no surprise to anybody when the word got around that Kelley had appeared in several episodes of *Ryan's Hope* the previous season—playing the vengeful stepdaughter of a wealthy plastic surgeon with a seamy past.

Nor had anybody been very surprised at the way the boys fell all over each other—trying to find out Kelley's name, her schedule, her phone number, her sign, *anything!* —when she first showed up at school.

And if, four weeks into the term, not one of Short Hills High School's hometown heroes had gotten anywhere near Kelley, nobody was too surprised at that, either.

Kelley was, simply, out of their league.

Which, of course—together with her beauty and her acting experience—made her the perfect Tracy Lord.

Well, not *quite* perfect. Kelley had been doing fine at portraying Tracy Lord's flawlessly polished exterior.

But so far, Tracy's interior—the flesh-and-blood vulnerability that Mike Connor brings to the surface in the play's second act—had completely escaped her.

Still, with six days left to go, Julie was confident she'd find a way to—

But did she have six days?

"I get to *kiss* Kelley Seaver?" asked Buckley, obviously thrilled at the very thought.

If a girl's pretty enough, thought Julie, *it doesn't matter if she's got the personality of a toxic dump. Boys will do anything to get next to her.*

But she reminded herself of a line from Shakespeare—*"The play's the thing!"*—and then she answered.

"Twice," she said.

"Son of a bitch!" said Buckley.

"Page twenty-seven," said Julie.

Eight

"How much Coke do you drink a day, anyway?" asks Patti Hamberger.

Patti, a thirteen-year-old friend of Sean's thirteen-year-old sister, Diana, is trying to start up a conversation.

She and Diana are sprawled out on the living-room floor, "studying" in front of the TV. It's about nine-thirty Wednesday night and Sean is on the return lap of his second Coke run since dinner.

Patti's caught him sneaking out of the kitchen and heading back to his room.

Ever since Diana told her big brother that her doe-eyed little friend had a mad crush on him, Sean has been doing his best to forget she ever mentioned it.

"About a gallon," Diana volunteers—obviously appalled and thoroughly disapproving.

"And you never get zits!" says Patti—as if Sean's zitlessness was the eighth wonder of the world.

Sean's beginning to feel sorry he ventured out of his room, starting to think he might have been happier staying in there and slowly dying of thirst, when the telephone rings and mercy-kills the conversation.

"I'll get it," says Diana.

As she hops to her feet, Patti tells Sean, "She hopes it's Timmy Evans."

"I do not," snaps Diana—blushing nonetheless—as she hurries across the room to the phone.

As she picks up the receiver, her little friend looks deep

into Sean's eyes and confides, "She's *hot* for Timmy Evans."

Sean tries not to think about what that means.

Diana darts a withering glance at her friend and then directs her attention to the telephone.

As if whoever it is at the other end of the line could see her, she smiles and says, "Hello?"

And then—bang!—just like that, her smile drops from her face.

Suddenly, terribly bored, she looks over at Sean and says, "Yes. He's here."

Sean wonders who's calling.

"Who shall I say is calling?" she asks.

Which, of course, is none of her damned business.

"Hey!" says Sean.

But before he can say anything more, his mother comes sailing out of her room, where she's been working out, doing aerobics and whatnot, and says, "Is that for me? Hi, Patti."

Her eyes on Sean, as she repeats the name that the caller has given her, Diana says, "Sara Beth Cavanaugh?"

Sean can't believe it! In fact, he *doesn't* believe it. This is obviously somebody's warped idea of a joke.

Like he *knows* it's a joke and he isn't about to fall for it, he looks at his sister and says, "Really?"

"Hi, Mrs. Manning," says Patti.

Diana—who hasn't the slightest idea who Sara Beth Cavanaugh is and couldn't care less anyway, since he's not Timmy Evans—tells her brother, "That's what she says."

Then, into the phone, she says, "Are you *really* Sara Beth Cavanaugh?"

Which *really* ticks Sean off.

Because what if it *is?*

What if, instead of waiting for him to call her and ask her if she's been not thinking about not going out with him—which he's been thinking about doing and meaning to do, ever since he got back from walking her home last Saturday—what if Sara Beth's decided to call him, instead?

"Damn it!" he says.

"Diana!" says his mother. "Give your brother the phone."

"Thank you," Sean tells his mother as he takes the phone from his sister.

"Don't be long, okay?" says his mother. "I'm expecting a call."

As she turns to go, Sean tells her, "Wait."

As his mother stops and turns to him, Sean lifts the phone to his ear and says, "Hi."

"Hi," says Sara Beth.

It's her. Without a doubt.

Sean's amazed. He's blown away.

But he's cool.

Right away, he asks Sara Beth if she'll hold on, while he gets to another phone.

Then, when Sara Beth says "Sure"—with his mother standing there as a witness—Sean asks his sister if she'd please hang up the phone for him when he picks up on the extension.

As if she were innocence itself, and she'd never think of listening in on her brother's phone call, Diana says, "Of course."

And then, as she takes the receiver from Sean, she adds, sweetly, "Would you like to use *my* phone?"

Without answering, Sean turns on his heels and heads for the extension in his sister's room.

Behind him, he hears his mother reminding his sister, "It's not *your phone*. It's just *in your room*."

"It's still *my room*!" Diana insists.

"*Diana!*" says his mother—meaning "Enough is enough."

As Sean steps inside his sister's room and starts to close

the door behind him, his mother catches his eye and reminds him, "Not too long, huh?"

Sean doesn't say a word. Although he'd like to. He'd like to tell all of them to get lost, to leave him the hell alone, to give him some goddamned room!

But Sara Beth is waiting.

And anyway, he's not that kind of guy. He wasn't raised to yell at women, no matter how much they annoy him or how crazy they make him.

So, he just looks from one of them to the other and then heaves a sigh and quietly but firmly closes the door.

It's dark in his sister's room. Which is just as well, considering what a mess it is.

In the moonlight that falls through his sister's window, Sean follows the telephone cord from the place where it plugs into the wall, across the floor, under the bed, and up onto a chair, where it disappears under a pile of stuff—clothes, records, books, and God only knows what else.

Digging the phone out from under the pile, he picks up the receiver and calls to his sister, "Thank you."

"My pleasure," she shouts back.

As he settles onto the floor and brings the receiver to his ear, Sean hears his sister clicking off the line, and then Sara Beth laughing.

"You have a little sister!" she says.

"Is that what it is?" says Sean.

"That's what it sounds like to me," says Sara Beth. "How old is she?"

"About as old as she's going to get, if she doesn't buzz off," says Sean. "Thirteen."

"That's a difficult age."

"You're telling me!"

She doesn't say anything to that. What is there to say?

Thinking he ought to say more, Sean comes up with, "I was just thinking about you."

Except he comes up with it at exactly the same time that

53

Sara Beth is saying, "I guess you're wondering why I'm calling?"

"No," says Sean, as Sara Beth says, "You were?"

"Yes," says Sean, as Sara Beth says, "You aren't wondering why I'm calling?"

"Yes, I am," says Sean. "But I guess you're calling about what I was thinking about. Which is your not thinking about our not going out sometime. Right?"

Sara Beth laughs and says, "Nope."

Sean feels a surge of embarrassment.

"I want to know if we're going to beat Horace Mann on Saturday."

"Oh," says Sean, relieved to be back on familiar ground. "Sure. If you like."

He wonders if he should tell her about the scout from Notre Dame.

"I like," says Sara Beth.

He decides he shouldn't.

"Done," says Sean.

"And," says Sara Beth, "now that you mention it, I have been not thinking about our not going out sometime, too."

"Oh, yeah?" says Sean. "That's great.

"So," he says, "what do you think?"

For a brief eternity, while Sean waits for her answer, Sara Beth says nothing.

Then she says, like she'd rather not, but can't help it, "I don't think Jack would understand."

It's kind of what Sean's been expecting.

Since last Saturday, all the dozens of times he's imagined this conversation, how it might go, he's always known how it probably would go.

But still, he'd always kind of hoped—

"If he knew," says Sara Beth.

If he knew!

"Yes," says Sean, tiptoeing over the minefield that's suddenly opened before him. "But what if he didn't know?

54

"I mean, what would there be to know? That we went for a walk? Or had coffee? Or caught a movie? I mean, what's that?"

"It *was* fun," Sara Beth admits,"being with somebody other than Marcy or Layla for a change."

"Thanks?"

She laughs.

"You know what I mean," she says.

"Sure," he tells her. "I get kind of tired of hanging out with the guys myself. Not that they're not good guys or anything. But it's not exactly stimulating."

"Am I?"

"Yeah," he says. "Am I?"

"What am I afraid of?" she says, more to herself than to him.

"I don't know," says Sean.

"There's nothing wrong with it, is there?"

"Not that I can see."

A moment passes.

And another.

"When were you thinking about?" she asks.

"I wasn't," Sean admits. "I mean, I hadn't got that far. But, well—"

He tells himself, *Why not?*

"How about Saturday night?"

"This Saturday?" asks Sara Beth.

"Yeah," says Sean. "I always have a hard time figuring out what to do at night, after a game. You know, go out and get blitzed with the guys. Or go home and veg out on TV."

"But hanging out with you—I mean, if I knew I was going to—going to *be,* I mean—hanging out with you— then that'd be—you know—okay."

He congratulates himself on being such a smooth talker.

"But Saturday night . . ." she says.

He can hear her wavering.

"We wouldn't have to go anyplace where anybody would see us," he tells her. "If that's what you're worried about.

"We could go someplace else. Make it a kind of test, you know?

"And then, that way, if everything's okay, which it will be, and you want to tell Jack about it, you can tell him you checked it out and it's no big thing, right?"

"Where would we go?" she asks him.

"To the movies?"

"As a test," she says.

"A free trial offer," Sean assures her.

"Well . . ."

He hears her take a breath, hears her let it out, hears her say, "Okay."

To himself, he says, *I'll be damned!*

To Sara Beth, he says, "So, I'll pick you up Saturday night?"

"Okay."

"Around seven o'clock?"

"Okay."

"Will you be at the game?"

"Okay. I mean, yes," she says. "Of course. I always go."

"Good," he says. "There's going to be a scout there. From Notre Dame. Looking me over."

"That's great!"

"Yeah," says Sean, wondering why he's told her and feeling embarrassed that he has. "Where?"

"My house."

"About seven?"

"Okay."

"And Sara Beth?"

"Yes?"

"Don't worry about it, okay?"

"Okay," she says. "And Sean?"

"Yes?"

"Good luck."

"Thanks."

"Good night, Sean."

"Good night, Sara Beth."

As he hangs up the phone, Sean just sits there a moment. He just sits there in the dark and feels himself grinning like a madman.

He tells himself it's no big deal. Come Saturday night, he and Sara Beth are just going to go out and catch a movie. So what?

So nothing. People do it all the time. It doesn't mean a thing.

So why is he sitting here in the dark, grinning like a madman? Huh?

And just who does he think he's kidding?

Nine

There's an old saying in the theater. It says, if you have a lousy dress rehearsal, you're sure to have a great show.

If there's any truth to it, Julie told herself, *I have nothing to worry about.*

She didn't wait for the curtain to close on the play's final scene. She shouted her review of the performance from her seat at the center of the empty auditorium.

"Rotten!" she shouted. "Amateurish!"

Sitting next to her, Patriciana nearly jumped out of his skin

"Well, it wasn't *wonderful,*" he conceded.

Wonderful? she thought. *With the sets falling down? The doors sticking? The cork getting stuck in the sherry bottle?*

Wonderful? With her leading lady, Kelley Seaver, projecting all the regal bearing of Princess Diana and all the warm vulnerability of Margaret Thatcher?

Wonderful? With Buckley—?

"Want to talk to them?" asked Patriciana.

"No," Julie decided.

It was a radical decision, she knew.

But with only six hours to go before they opened in front of an auditorium filled with paying customers, there was nothing she could say to her actors that she hadn't already said to them a hundred times before.

Whatever last-minute reminders she had for them, she could save for her pep talk, just before the curtain. Right now, they'd probably profit most if she gave them a chance to stew in their own juices for a while.

As Julie got up from her seat, Patriciana said, "What should I tell them?"

"Repent!" said Julie. Squeezing past him, she made her way to the aisle.

"That's all?" asked Patriciana.

"No," said Julie.

She had to do *something* about Buckley.

Patriciana agreed.

"Buckley?" he guessed.

"Yes," said Julie.

"Shoot him?" asked Patriciana.

"Tell him to meet me in the cafeteria," she said.

"Ah!" said Patriciana approvingly. *"Poison him."*

"Rehearse him," said Julie. "That's where I'll be, if you need me."

She turned and hurried up the aisle. Reaching the door, she paused and turned back to Patriciana.

"But, Bob," she called.

He was halfway down the aisle by now, headed backstage. He stopped and turned to her.

"Don't need me," she concluded.

Then she turned and headed out the door.

As she moved down the empty corridor, heading for the cafeteria, she told herself, *It's got to get better, 'cause it can't get worse.*

She'd been wrong about Buckley.

Dead wrong.

He was as smart as she'd hoped. Smarter. He'd learned all his lines, letter-perfect, overnight.

And he could be funny. In exactly the chip-on-the-shoulder way Mike Connor was supposed to be funny.

And cute? Yes, he was cute. But what good did it do him? None.

Because, as cute and funny and as smart as he was,

when it came to women—and especially when it came to Kelley Seaver—Buckley was totally helpless. Nowhere. Nerdly.

Of course, right from the start, Julie expected Buckley might have a little trouble dominating Kelley Seaver. After all, so far as Julie knew, in real life nobody ever had.

She also expected Buckley to be a little awkward and embarrassed kissing Kelley. Strange as it may seem, making an on-stage kiss seem natural is one of the hardest things for an actor to do.

But with practice—of which there'd been plenty, these last five days and nights—Julie had felt sure these minor problems would go away.

Except they hadn't. The first time Buckley was introduced to Kelley he'd been completely overwhelmed by her and, up to this moment, he still hadn't recovered.

And the kiss!

God! You could see Buckley working up his courage for the lousy kiss from the moment he walked on stage, early in the first act, until the moment he actually got to it, deep in the second act.

It was like he'd never kissed a girl before.

Which, when Julie thought about it, might even be the case.

When she thought about it—much too late in the game—it occurred to Julie that she'd never heard of Buckley going out with anybody.

Not that he didn't date, or spend some time hanging out with one girl or another. It was just that, so far as Julie could discover, it was never any one girl.

Or, if he did see a lot of any one girl, she was likely to be one of those girls that boys hang out with, but hardly ever go out with.

Julie knew the type. All too well. She *was* the type. It was, she told herself, the type she'd chosen to be.

But she didn't have time to think about that now.

60

Now was the time to turn Buckley around. This was her one last chance to bring out all the overbearing masculinity she knew Buckley had in him, her final crack at turning Buckley into a reasonable facsimile of Tracy Lord's savior and everybody's favorite chauvinist pig, Mike Connor.

Entering the cafeteria, Julie set to work, moving chairs and tables around, positioning them so they'd approximate the furniture on the set for Mike and Tracy's big love scene.

The love scene was the key to the whole play. If she could make that work, the play would work.

But how? The truth was, she had no idea what she'd do with Buckley, once he arrived. Over the last five days, she'd tried everything short of—

"Hi, Doc," said Buckley.

He was standing in the doorway, watching Julie arranging the furniture.

"Setting up for a wake?"

Jesus! thought Julie. *He looks like his dog just died!*

"Kelley hasn't been giving you much help," she told him.

It was, she told herself, at least half the truth.

"God, she's beautiful," said Buckley, shaking his head. "But I don't seem to be making much of an impression on her, do I?"

"Because she's *Kelley!*" said Julie. "If you'd think of her as *Tracy*—"

"But she's *not* Tracy!" Buckley insisted. For a moment, he looked like he might burst into tears.

Quickly, averting his gaze, he dropped his eyes to the floor.

Poor baby! thought Julie.

Taking a deep breath, she walked over to him and put her hand on his shoulder.

"Hey," she said, very softly, very calmly.

After a moment, Buckley looked up at her.

61

"You know," Julie told him, very softly, very calmly, "they're just girls, Kelley and Tracy...

"And you're just boys, Mike and you...

"And sometimes...

She pressed the palm of her hand to Buckley's chest and looked deep into his eyes.

"Sometimes," she continued, her voice sounding a little husky in her ears, "boys and girls...

"It doesn't matter who they are...

"Or where they are...

"Or what's going on around them...

"They just want each other...

"So much...

"They—"

He kissed her.

As she'd been begging him to.

For the sake of the show, she told herself.

Only...

It felt so good, kissing him!

So good, with his mouth—so hungry—pressed to her mouth!

With his arms—so long and strong—wrapped around her!

With his body—his breath coming deep and slow—pressed against hers!

"Mm..." she murmured—when, at last, the kiss was ended.

For a moment, she just looked at him.

And then she raised her face to be kissed again.

And this time...

It seemed to last forever...

And, yet, it ended all too soon!

"Mm..."

She nestled her cheek against his chest.

She couldn't believe what she was feeling!

She wouldn't believe it!

She'd gotten carried away, playing the part. That was all.

It had to be!

For a moment, basking in the warmth of Buckley's embrace, Julie said nothing.

But then, after a moment, she whispered his name—not *Buckley's* name, but *his* name.

She called him Mike.

And then, just as she'd hoped, Buckley whispered *her* name.

He called her Tracy.

And then they were playing the scene, speaking the lines and feeling the feelings—as if she were Tracy Lord and he were Mike Connor.

All of a sudden, in the wake of Mike's kiss, Tracy seemed to have the shakes.

So did Mike.

Tracy wondered what it was that had shaken her so.

Mike thought it might be love.

Tracy said it *couldn't* be.

And yet . . .

Mike started to kiss her again.

And Tracy seemed willing.

But suddenly, as if she'd heard a startling sound, she broke away from him.

Someone was coming!

Mike cursed.

"Good!" said Julie, calling an end to the scene they were playing.

What was that! she wondered.

"You're a good kisser," she told Buckley—like she was a teacher, grading his paper.

Like she hadn't been surprised—amazed—by what she'd felt when he kissed her.

"Yeah," said Buckley, smiling shyly.

She hoped he hadn't gotten the wrong idea!

"Well," said Buckley, "I'm glad *you* think so, anyway."

He was still thinking about Kelley!

"I'm not Kelley," Julie admitted.

"No," said Buckley.

The swine!

"But I'm not exactly chopped liver, either," she reminded him.

"No," he said, smiling. "Not *exactly.*"

She laughed.

What else could she do?

"Want to try it again?" she dared him.

"Sure," he said.

She smiled.

"Too bad," she said, "I've got to run over the lighting cues."

Buckley laughed.

Quickly, Julie turned and headed for the door.

"Thanks," he called to her.

Pausing in the doorway, like Lauren Bacall in *To Have and Have Not,* Julie smiled and lifted an eyebrow and drawled, "The pleasure was all mine."

Buckley laughed again, as she turned and went out the door.

Wow! she told herself as she hurried down the corridor. *What some people won't do, just to get a good performance out of an actor.*

Ten

The crowd comes to its feet cheering as Sean leads the Kenyon Crusaders out onto the field.

As they jog over to their warm-up area, most of Sean's teammates steal glances at the stands, trying to catch sight of their friends or their girls—or whoever—in the crowd.

But not Sean. The crowd's roar is his signal to begin pretending there is no crowd.

At the moment the cheering begins, he begins shrinking the size of his world, until there is no world outside the boundaries of the playing field.

Usually, anyway.

But today, as the crowd cheers, Sean finds himself sifting through the voices, listening for Sara Beth's voice among them.

It's foolish, he knows. But just trying gives him an excuse to imagine Sara Beth up on her feet and shouting his name.

For an instant, as he imagines her, Sean is Bruce Springsteen, taking the stage at Madison Square Garden.

He is King Arthur, spurring his battle stallion out onto the field of battle.

He is . . . laughing at himself and his fevered imagination.

And then, in the next instant, the very idea of Sara Beth —the picture of her in his mind's eye—disappears without a trace.

Nor does the idea of a big-time college-football scout—

sitting in the stands, watching him, judging him—rise to take its place.

In Sean's mind there is no longer room for such extraneous thoughts.

There is only the game and the playing of it.

From the beginning it's a good game.

Horace Mann's offense is organized around Harlon Avery, who stands six feet two and weighs two hundred twenty pounds.

In his junior year and still growing, Harlon is already fast enough to run around you and strong enough to run over you and competitor enough to prefer the latter.

Over the course of the afternoon, he scores five times for his team.

But it isn't enough.

Early in the fourth quarter, Sean sends his right end, Richie Boynton, on a fly pattern, hits him with a clothesline pass thirty yards down the field, and watches him sprint, unmolested, across Horace Mann's goal line.

When Escabedo adds the point after, Kenyon moves on top, 42–35.

Later in the quarter, Sean adds another touchdown for insurance. As his big fullback sweeps right, Sean fakes handing off to him, hides the ball on his own hip, runs to his left, and takes off on a twenty-six-yard jaunt that carries him all the way into the end zone.

When the game is over, Kenyon has won, 48–35.

After four games, they are 4–0 and still tied with Hoover in the race for the league championship.

And Don Jellinek is impressed.

"Fine game," he tells Sean.

He shakes his hand and smiles and looks Sean in the eye.

Sean is surprised by Jellinek's appearance, but he tries not to let it show.

They are standing in the locker room, in front of Sean's

locker—Jellinek and Sean and the coach. The coach has just finished making the introductions.

Sean is thinking that Jellinek doesn't look much like the smooth-talking representative of the Good Life that he was expecting.

A wiry little guy with crew-cut white hair, a weathered face, and flinty eyes, he looks more like somebody you'd call Doc.

On the spot, putting aside his preconceptions, Sean finds himself liking this man and wanting to be liked by him.

With the coach looking on—beaming like an exhibitor at a dog show—Sean shakes Jellinek's hand, meets his gaze, and tells him, "Thanks. I appreciate it."

"Do you suppose you and me and your dad could sit down somewhere, and talk a little about your plans for the future?"

"Sure," Sean tells him. "My father suggested, if you wanted to talk, he would meet you at Mitch's on Broadway and Eighty-second and I could join you as soon as I've showered and dressed."

Jellinek smiles.

"He's a planner, your father," he says.

With a nod and smile, Sean agrees.

"You've got that right," he says.

"Good quarterbacks don't just happen," says Jellinek.

"You can say that again," says the coach.

Acknowledging the coach's contribution with a nod, Jellinek tells Sean, "Mitch's will be fine. Broadway and . . . ?"

"Eighty-second," Sean reminds him.

"You can't miss it," says the coach.

And he doesn't.

When Sean walks into Mitch's Café about forty-five minutes later, he discovers Jellinek sharing a booth with his father in a relatively quiet back corner of the dining room.

Standing unobserved on the dining room's threshold, Sean takes a moment to study his father.

This is Frank Manning's big moment, the moment he's been dreaming about ever since he bought his son his first kid-size football and showed him how to grip it in his kid-size hand.

Now is the moment when Frank gets his chance to set his son on the high road to success and maybe fortune and just possibly fame.

Although it may have been a fantasy when it started, for years now—probably since his career at the bank peaked at the middle-upper level, and certainly since his wife asked him, please, to pack his things and go—Frank Manning has practically lived for this moment.

And now that the moment is finally here, Sean can't remember the last time he saw his father looking so happy or so much at ease.

Standing there, looking across the room at his father, Sean is grateful that he's had the good fortune to give him this moment, this piece of his dream.

But at the same time, he's also terribly aware that the rest of his father's dream could very easily stretch out and snare him from the next moment to the end of his life.

In fact, Sean is wondering if he shouldn't just turn around and melt back into the crowd and disappear, when his father spots him.

Returning his father's smile, Sean waves and crosses the room and joins his father and Don Jellinek in their booth.

"I've been telling your father you looked pretty good out there today," says Jellinek.

He says it like it's a compliment, but Sean understands it's really an honest assessment of his performance.

He wasn't great today. He was good. Pretty good. As Jellinek says. As Sean agrees.

Meeting Jellinek's gaze and returning his smile, Sean says, "We were pretty lucky."

"The good ones make their own luck," says his father.

"Seems like," says Jellinek, nodding his agreement.

And then, to Sean, he says, "I don't want to keep you long. I imagine you've got plans."

"Yes," says Sean.

"What's her name?" asks his father. "Sara Beth?"

Immediately, Sean is sorry he told his father anything about his plans for tonight.

"Dad," he says.

"Daughter of Francis X. Cavanaugh," his father tells Jellinek. "You've heard of Cavanaugh Construction?"

"I think so," says Jellinek, sounding more polite than persuasive.

"They do a lot of business with us at the bank."

Jellinek nods and says, "Well. So as not to keep a lady waiting . . ."

And with that, he begins telling Sean and his father about Notre Dame, about the opportunities it offers its student athletes—the educational opportunities, the social opportunities, the career opportunities.

It isn't a sales talk. He tells it straight and, living up to his word, he keeps it short and sweet.

He doesn't offer Sean a scholarship, right on the spot. Instead, he suggests that Sean and his father might want to give some thought to flying out to South Bend, sometime after Christmas.

As the guests of Notre Dame, they could take a look around and meet some of the people who run the football program and see for themselves if Notre Dame isn't the kind of school they're looking for.

Notre Dame would pick up all the expenses, of course, and there would be no obligation. That's understood.

"Think about it," he says, as he gets up to leave.

Shaking Sean's hand, he says, "Stay healthy."

"Nice to meet you, Frank," he tells his father. "I'll stay in touch."

"Nice meeting you, Don," says Sean's father. "And please do."

"Thanks," says Sean.

Jellinek nods and, dropping a five-dollar bill on the table to cover the cost of his drink, he's gone.

As soon as he clears the room, Frank Manning looks across the table at his son, and—scowling and pointing at him, like an old Uncle Sam poster—he says, "Notre Dame Wants You!"

And he laughs.

And he reaches across the table and takes Sean's hand and squeezes it.

And he looks Sean in the eye.

And Sean can see tears of joy welling in his eyes, as he says, "And Notre Dame is just the first. There's lots more to come. We're on our way!"

For a split second, Sean has a nearly irresistible urge to laugh and look his father straight in the eye and say, "What do you mean 'we,' Keemosabe?"

But there's no way he could bring himself to spoil his father's big moment.

So he smiles.

And he nods.

And he says, "Yeah."

Eleven

The drumbeat of the rain, the sting of the raindrops pelting against her upraised face—this, Julie had to remind herself, was neither.

This was the shower in the girls' locker room, downstairs from the auditorium where—in about half an hour—the curtain would be going up on *The Short Hills High School Dramatic Society's Production of Philip Barry's* The Philadelphia Story, *a Comedy in Three Acts*.

In just a few minutes, the ushers would be opening the doors to the auditorium and showing the audience—including Miles Hanna, the drama critic of *The Short Hills Register* and *The Blade*'s Jon Crowley and her own parents and the parents of her friends *and her enemies!*—to their seats.

But Julie didn't want to think about any of them or any of that, now.

She'd just extricated herself from the last of a series of last-minute crises that had kept her hopping from the moment she walked out of the cafeteria, wondering what in the world she was doing, necking with Roy Buckley, in the middle of the afternoon, before the evening of—!

She shook her head.

She didn't want to think about *that* right now, either!

She didn't want to think about anything.

This was the proverbial calm before the proverbial storm and she wanted to enjoy every last second of it, for as long as she could.

And how long is that? she wondered.

Opening her eyes, she squinted through the pelting rain and checked out the time on her trusty—water-resistant to 50 meters—Casio.

It was pushing seven-thirty. Storm time was fast approaching. Calm time was over.

Quickly turning off the shower, she grabbed a towel from a pile near the door and hurried out into the locker room.

Stepping over her discarded sweatshirt and jeans, which lay crumpled on the floor where she'd dropped them only a few seconds ago, she hurried over to the locker where she'd stowed the opening-night outfit that she'd brought with her from home the first thing this morning.

Hurrying, she toweled herself dry, squeezed into her panty hose, and stepped into the clingy black silk jersey dress she'd borrowed from her mother to wear tonight.

She supposed it was odd of her not to own a dress of her own—except for a sundress she'd had to get, back in June, so she wouldn't look too out of place at a distant cousin's lawn-party wedding.

But the way she saw it, putting on a dress and makeup and jewelry was what girls did to attract the attention of boys.

And she wasn't much interested in attracting the attention of boys who were attracted by dresses and makeup and jewelry.

She dressed for herself.

She wore jeans, mostly, with boots or running shoes.

And lots of different tops—all of them nice, and each of them, for one reason or another, interesting in its own way.

She wore her hair short and close-cut. She kept it clean and shining. She showered daily, bathed often, and had no aversion to bath salts, body oils, and subtle perfumes.

But that was it.

That was Julie.

Take her or leave her.

Because, if her experiences so far had taught her anything, it was that most boys weren't worth the all-out effort most girls put into attracting them.

Particularly if they happened to be jocks. They were the worst. Although it had taken her forever to realize it.

Back in ninth and tenth grades, she'd gone through a regular jock phase. It had been part of her search for a tough guy with the soul of a poet.

But none of the jocks she went out with had anything like the soul of a poet. Instead, what they had, every single one of them, was this born-to-win attitude that turned their relationships into contests, the girls they went out with into opponents, and their opponents' body parts into trophies.

After a while, Julie'd had enough of jocks and their games.

By the time she'd finished her sophomore year, she'd benched herself.

For good.

She sighed and stepped into her black calf pumps.

She fastened the freshwater-pearl pendant with the antique gold chain—which her mother had loaned her for good luck—around her neck and turned to look at herself in the mirror.

"Oh, Chubbo!" she said, shaking her head at the ripe-to-bursting creature she saw reflected in the mirror. "Talk about T and A! You've got the national endowment!"

Although her mother's dress fell softly—like a caress —over her mother's perfect figure, in its struggle to contain her own embarrassment of riches it was stretched thin.

Nudity, she told herself, *would be less revealing and more modest.*

Still, what could she do?

Nothing.

Quickly, using the comb that her mother had been thoughtful enough to pack inside the black calf purse that she'd been kind enough to let her daughter borrow for the night, Julie combed out her still-damp hair.

Then, after a fast glance in the mirror, she took off, clattering her heels over the locker room's tiled floor, hitting the brakes and skidding out the door.

A few moments later, she was backstage, telling the cast their work was over and now was the time to relax and enjoy themselves.

All they had to do, she told them, was trust the play to carry them through, and, she added, "Remember everything I've taught you."

With that, she turned and gave Buckley a big juicy wink and said, "Especially you."

And then, while everybody giggled and Buckley blushed, she told them they were going to be wonderful and headed for the wings.

And a few moments after that, as the houselights dimmed for the start of *The Philadelphia Story*, she was standing at the back of the auditorium, praying they wouldn't make a liar out of her.

Twelve

He catches her peeking at him through the curtain. She smiles, lets the curtain fall back into place, and then opens the door to him.

He says, "Hi, Sara Beth."

And she probably says, "Hi, Sean."

But he isn't paying attention to what she says. He's too knocked out by how she looks. She looks incredible!

She's wearing a chamois cowgirl dress that drapes over and clings to every well-defined inch of her body, from its open neck down to its fringed hem.

On her feet are high-heeled Western boots and at her ears are real turquoise earrings that peek out from under her raven hair and pick up the color of her flashing sea-green eyes.

And her smile, Sara Beth's smile, is so warm and wide, Sean could just reach out and—

"Maid's night off," she tells him, as she stands aside and motions him into the house.

He laughs at her joke.

But the moment he sets foot inside her door and finds himself standing in her perfectly appointed, turn-of-the-century foyer, he realizes she probably isn't joking.

She shows him down the hallway, past the richly furnished living room and into an oak-and-leather recreation room that she calls the den.

She tells him she's sorry her parents aren't here for him

to meet, but, she explains, they've flown off to Palm Springs for the weekend.

Instantly, Sean finds himself wondering if he and Sara Beth have the house to themselves.

And he wonders, if they do have the house to themselves, how long do they have it for?

And then he laughs at himself for what he's thinking. And because he's amazed at how easily he's forgotten that Sara Beth is "taken," that she's Jack Ramsey's girl.

"What's so funny?" Sara Beth asks him.

"I've forgotten," says Sean.

Sara Beth looks at him like he's a little strange, which he probably is. She's dropped into an oversize leather armchair and stretched her feet out on the oversize leather ottoman that stands in front of it.

Sean sits on the leather couch, opposite her.

Remembering her manners, she says, "Can I get you anything?"

"No, thanks," says Sean. "It's pretty late, if we're going to get to an eight o'clock show."

He takes *The New York Post* out from under his arm, apologizes for bringing the trashy tabloid into her house, and opens it to the "Movie Clock."

"Which," he tells her, "unfortunately, happens to be the best list of films and starting times available on my local newstand."

"Aren't you going to tell me?" she says.

"What?" he asks her.

"Notre Dame," she reminds him.

"Oh," he says. "Are you really interested?"

She looks at him like he's crazy.

"Of course I'm interested," she tells him.

Which kind of surprises him and kind of pleases him and definitely persuades him to fold up the paper and tell her about Jellinek.

He makes it short and sweet for her—as Jellinek made

76

it for him—and when he's done, she says, "That's fantastic!"

"Yeah," says Sean. "It's nice that they want me. Now, what about helping me find a movie?"

As he opens the *Post* to the "Movie Clock," she says, "Don't you think it's fantastic?"

Resigning himself to looking at the bright side, but not wanting to make too much of it, Sean looks up from the paper and says, "Well, it *does* mean, if I want to go to college, I won't have to go in the city and live at home with my mother and sister for the next four years.

"So, yeah," he says. "That is pretty fantastic, I guess. To know that. Sure."

Then, thinking he's answered her question, Sean takes another shot at the "Movie Clock."

"*Pretty* fantastic?" she says. "Don't you realize what playing football—what being the starting quarterback at a school like Notre Dame—can mean for your future?"

Sean can't believe how seriously and personally she's taking all this.

"I think I can," he tells her.

But that doesn't seem to satisfy Sara Beth.

Getting up from her chair, she crosses the room and perches on the edge of the couch next to Sean.

And then, as if she were confiding a major secret to him, she says, "According to Jack, if you're a college athlete and a good student and attractive and well-spoken, you start out on an inside track that runs straight from the campus to the boardrooms of the biggest corporations in America."

"Oh?" says Sean.

"Yes," she says. "You look at the people who sit on the boards of directors and you'll see that a lot of them are former college athletes."

"Ah," says Sean.

He can't believe how serious Sara Beth's gotten. In fact, it's so sudden and so surprising, he can't help but laugh.

"Jesus!" he says. "You and Jack ought to be running Notre Dame's recruitment program. You two could sure teach Don Jellinek a thing or two!"

"I don't get it," Sara Beth confesses. "Isn't that what you want? To be successful?"

Sean smiles and shrugs and says, "Could be. I don't know."

"Well," she says, "what do you think?"

"Me?" says Sean. "I think I want to see a movie."

He ducks into the *Post*.

Sara Beth tugs at his sleeve.

"With your life?" she asks.

"I don't know," he says.

"Well," she says, "what do you like doing?"

"Finally!" he says. "A question I can answer."

And so he tells her. In no special order. Just as it comes to him.

"Taking pictures. Thinking up stories about the people in them.

"Listening to music. Especially in a car, driving somewhere, late at night.

"Walks in the woods and in out-of-the-way places that I don't usually get to in the city—the flower market, the Ukranian church.

"Food. Dancing. Good people.

"Sleeping late. Skinny-dipping. Making love. . . .

"Movies!" says Sara Beth.

"Love 'em," he tells her.

"What time is it?" she asks.

He looks at the cheap Casio that he's been wearing since his real watch died.

He sees that it's water resistant to 50 meters and that the time is 7:54.

"We blew it," he tells her.

She laughs and says, "Perfect!"

"Why?" he asked her.

"Because," she told him, "going to a movie is no way to celebrate."

"Celebrate what?"

"Notre Dame!"

"My alma mater."

"We should go dancing."

"Sure," he tells her. "Where?"

She's got an idea—an idea that delights her and sets her eyes blazing and brings her to her feet.

"*I* know!" she says. "You wait here, okay?"

She turns and heads for the door.

"Wait!" he calls after her. "Where are you going?"

Reaching the door, she pauses and turns back to him.

"Upstairs," she says. "To make reservations and change."

"Change?"

"It will only take a second," she tells him. "You'll need a tie. You can borrow one of Daddy's. Do you know how to do them or do you need a ready-made?"

"I don't need a ready-made," he tells her. "But this place we're going . . . ?"

"It's my party," she assures him.

But her assurance has the opposite effect.

"What kind of place . . . ?"

"Trust me," she tells him. "You'll love it."

"I will?"

"You have to," she insists with a smile. "It happens to be one of those out-of-the-way places that you usually don't get to in the city."

"Oh!" he says like he finally knows what she's talking about. Although he doesn't. But at least she's been listening.

She nods, as if everything is all cleared up and then she turns and walks off.

For a moment, Sean watches after her and wonders what he's gotten himself into.

Then she calls to him from down the hall.

"If you want a drink," she says, "help yourself. I don't know if they'll serve us where we're going."

"Thanks!" he calls back to her.

He turns and looks at the well-stocked little wet bar in the corner of the room.

Ordinarily, he's not a drinking man. But this is turning out to be an occasion.

He asks himself what the great W. C. Fields might say at a time like this, faced with the decision he's facing.

"Don't mind if I do," he drawls.

And he sidles over to the dispensary.

Thirteen

Raising her glass, beautiful Tracy Lord smiled at handsome Mike Connor.

Handsome Mike Connor smiled at beautiful Tracy Lord and raised his glass.

Standing at the back of the jam-packed auditorium, Julie braced herself.

This was it, for all the marbles. Tracy Lord's older brother, Sandy, had just departed the Lord family's patio and left Tracy alone in the moonlight with Mike Connor. Tracy and Mike, a.k.a. Kelley and Buckley, were easing into their love scene.

If Mike Connor didn't sweep Tracy Lord off her feet, if his kiss didn't knock her socks off, then—no matter how admirably the rest of the play was directed and performed —the show, as a whole, just wouldn't make it.

On the other hand, if somehow Mike Connor *did* sweep Tracy Lord off her feet, if by some miracle his kiss *did* knock her socks off, then the play—as old as it was— could and just might take off and fly.

That's why, ever since the cafeteria, when she'd done her damnedest to get a rise out of Buckley, Julie had done everything she could think of to keep him pumped up for this scene. Like singling him out when she gave the cast her final pep talk just before the curtain.

Then, after that, when the first act was over and she rushed backstage to tell everybody they were doing fine and keep it up, she paid a visit to Buckley's dressing room.

She knocked on his door and popped her head inside and caught him, standing in the middle of the floor, half-way through changing costumes and bare to the waist.

She didn't say a word, at first. She just looked him up and down.

And then, she smiled a slow smile and said, "Foxy!"

And then she popped her head back out the door.

She thought she saw a little leer in the smile on Buckley's face, in the split second before she closed the door behind her.

She hoped so.

Because, if ever in his life there was a time for Buckley to feel like a real macho man and a certified hunk, now was the time.

Julie crossed her fingers and held her breath.

With Buckley and Kelley exchanging small talk and banter, the love scene started out fine.

Then, as their small talk and banter escalated into verbal sparring, things started getting a little more serious.

Now, Mike and Tracy were teasing and toying with each other—acting aggressive, but being flirtatious.

And still the acting held up.

Then, suddenly, Tracy was challenging Mike—almost daring him to kiss her.

And he did.

Buckley took Kelley in his arms. No. He *swept her up* in his arms! And kissed her! But really *kissed her!*

From the way Kelley reacted—snapping as taut as a bowstring in Buckley's rough embrace—Julie guessed that Buckley had surprised her with his tongue.

As the kiss ended, Kelley stood there, bug-eyed and dumbstruck, just staring at Buckley.

Like she was *supposed* to. But like she never had *before*. Like she had been *blown away!*

Buckley didn't wait for her to raise her face to be kissed again. He *couldn't* wait!

Cupping her face in his hands, he leaned down to her, lifted her mouth to his and kissed her again.

And this time, between Buckley's flaming desire and Kelley's smoldering anger, there was *real passion* in the kiss.

Maybe it wasn't exactly the kind of passion that Philip Barry had in mind when he wrote the scene, fifty years back, but from where Julie was standing, it was the next best thing and a real godsend.

Buckley's done it! she thought.

But what about Kelley?

As stunned as she'd been and as furious as she was, would she remember to act?

For a moment, while Kelley held her tongue, Julie held her breath.

But then Kelley's automatic pilot must have cut in, because—in a voice that dripped with *real astonishment*—she whispered Mike Connor's name.

Like she was *supposed* to. But like she never had *before*. Like she'd been *wiped out!*

Fantastic! thought Julie.

Transfixed, she stood watching as the scene picked up from there and practically soared to its conclusion.

And when, at the end of the scene, Tracy and Mike ran off to the pool for their moonlight dip, Julie joined in with the audience and sent them on their way, riding on a wave of enthusiastic applause.

How she wished she was Tracy, running off for her moment with Mike!

Did she wish she was Kelley, too? Did she wish Buckley had kissed her?

That way? With all that passion?

Twice?

Of course not! she told herself. *Don't be stupid!*

" *'The play's the thing,'* " she reminded herself.

And she put the thought aside.

And meanwhile, up on the stage, just as Philip Barry intended, the energy of the love scene picked up the play and propelled it straight through the ensuing complications of the plot, through the remainder of the second act and on through the third act to the play's surefire conclusion.

And when at last the curtain closed on Tracy Lord's happy ending, the audience rose to its feet, applauding and whistling and cheering.

"Bravo!" shouted Julie, feeling not the slightest bit embarrassed about adding her voice to the chorus of congratulations.

As the cast took bow after bow, she made her way down the aisle, clapping her hands and shouting along with the crowd, "Bravo!" to the boys and "Brava!" to the girls.

And then, before she knew it, *she* was up on the stage, enjoying *her own* happy ending, basking in the warmth of the stage lights and floating, free of care, on the sweet sound of success.

Fourteen

Floating at the top of Rockefeller Center, just a step down from the stars and sixty stories above the winking lights of the city below, the Stardust Room is like a joke.

It's like one of those swank supper clubs you see in movies from the thirties—the kind of place where Fred Astaire and Ginger Rogers used to spend their evenings, sipping champagne and tap-dancing their brains out.

Except, of course, Fred and Ginger aren't here tonight, because this happens to be fifty years later. Only nobody here seems to have noticed.

Not the maître d' who greeted Sean and Sara Beth at the door. Not the captain who showed them to their table. Not any of the waiters who've been fluttering around them since they first sat down.

None of the people sitting at the other tables seems to have noticed, either. All decked out in their formal and semiformal best, most of them look like they got themselves laminated sometime back in the thirties.

And out on the dance floor, the story isn't any different. It's nineteen thirty-something out there too, as Bobby Rosengarden and His Orchestra take one "musical stroll down Memory Lane" after another, and the dancers cruise through fox-trots and jitterbugs—and even exotic rhumbas and cha-chas—without batting an eye or missing a beat.

In fact, the illusion of yesteryear conjured up by this dazzling, Art Deco wedding cake of a room is so persuasive that Sean felt from the moment he walked in like he'd actually passed through a time warp and entered into Another Dimension of Reality!

"Act natural" was the first thing Sara Beth said to him when she led him out of the elevator and he saw where she'd brought him.

And then, as they approached the maître d', when Sara Beth saw that Sean was about to burst out laughing and blow the whole deal, she clutched his arm and whispered, "Pretend you're one of them."

Wiping the grin off his face, Sean glanced over at Sara Beth, nodded, and said, "Groovy."

But passing for one of them hadn't been as easy for him as it was for Sara Beth. For one thing, Sara Beth wasn't wearing running shoes.

And she didn't have a silk tie knotted around the neck of her plaid sportshirt, either.

And more to the point, in her formfitting black velvet cocktail dress, with her hair swept up off her bare shoulders and her mother's diamond earrings dangling from her ears, she didn't look much like your average, underaged high school kid, either.

In fact, she looked so fabulous, a man would have to be a blind man or a fool to make an issue of her age.

Luckily, the maître d' at the Stardust Room was neither. He'd been so knocked out by Sara Beth, he'd barely had the presence of mind to give Sean's outfit the contemptuous glance it so richly deserved, before he passed them along to his captain for seating.

From there on in, it had been a cinch.

Sean and Sara Beth had sat down at their table and studied the menu.

Deciding to skip the first four courses and go directly to dessert, they'd ordered champagne and strawberries, flown in fresh from South America and served with *crème fraîche*.

Then, at Sara Beth's suggestion, the first thing Sean did

when their order arrived was raise his glass in a toast to Don Jellinek and Notre Dame.

Once that was done, they'd sat back and sipped champagne like Fred and Ginger and nibbled strawberries and tried—without much success—not to laugh or crack a smile at all the incredibly unbelievable fuddihood around them.

It was a fantastic joke while it lasted.

But after a while Sara Beth reminded Sean that dancing was supposed to be one of his favorite things to do.

Of course, slow dancing hadn't been what Sean had in mind when he said that. What he'd meant was—

But Sara Beth knew what he meant and, nonetheless, she was asking him to take her out on the dance floor and join in with all the frisky museum pieces and premature antiques who were already out there cutting a rug.

Which was kind of a joke, too. And kind of a dare, as well. And not a bad idea—at least as far as Sean could see at the time.

Except, just a second ago—after Sean smiled at the joke and took the dare and got up from the table and escorted Sara Beth to the dance floor—a funny thing happened.

What happened when Sean and Sara Beth reached the dance floor and Sara Beth turned to face Sean—at the moment her eyes met his and just before she came into his arms and they began to dance—wasn't funny.

In fact, it was so like a dream come true that Sean couldn't quite believe it.

"Do you believe it?" he asks Sara Beth.

He feels her hair against his cheek, her head against his shoulder, her body moving against his.

Sara Beth laughs and says, "It *isn't* the kind of place you usually get to, right?"

Which isn't an answer to the question Sean was asking her. He was talking about dreams coming true, because he

87

was feeling like maybe they could. In fact, he was feeling like maybe a dream was coming true, right here and right now.

But Sara Beth's misunderstanding his question brings Sean back to his senses. He reminds himself that he's been drinking. And then he reminds himself that Sara Beth belongs to Jack Ramsey. And then he says, "No, it isn't like the kind of places I usually get to. It's beautiful."

Sara Beth looks at him like he's crazy.

And maybe he is.

Because, all of a sudden, with Sara Beth in his arms, he realizes that he is, quite literally, floating on air, sky-high above the clouds and dancing among the stars.

And he wonders if this is what it feels like to be in love.

Fifteen

They went sailing through the night, Patriciana behind the wheel of his ancient VW Beetle convertible, and Julie, blowing in the breeze, beside him.

They'd stayed behind to close up the auditorium, and now they were on their way to the cast party at Angelo's Villa Bella.

Luckily, it was a clear night, because Patriciana's Bug —which he'd christened "Go-Go Dancer"—was, as the name implied, topless.

It wasn't far from school to Angelo's, and after a few bone-chilling minutes, they arrived.

After Patriciana found a sheltered spot to park, he gave Julie his arm and escorted her across the parking lot and into the restaurant.

At the rear of the restaurant, beyond the main dining room and bar, Angelo's Private Party Room was jam-packed with members of the cast and crew, their dates and guests, and the usual complement of school officials and chaperons.

Everybody was busy eating and drinking and dancing and horsing around. But when Julie and Patriciana appeared at the door, it seemed as if everybody noticed them at the same time.

As if on cue, everybody in the room dropped what they were doing, turned to the door, and greeted them with cheers and whistles, bravos and applause.

Overwhelmed at first, after a moment Julie and Patriciana joined in, first applauding each other and then applauding everyone who was applauding them.

Then, as the applause peaked and faded, they stepped inside the room and joined the party.

And what a party it was!

There was food.

Julie was famished. And she didn't care if filling up on Angelo's famous linguine carbonara made her mother's dress burst at the seams.

There was drink.

A single glass of red wine, smuggled to her by a cute young waiter who hadn't yet learned the language or the state liquor laws.

And there was dancing.

Which Julie loved—even though, feeling as wiped-out as she did in the wake of her debut as a Dramatic Society director, she didn't really have the energy she needed to throw herself into it like she usually did.

And, finally, there was Buckley.

Julie had seen him backstage, after the show.

She'd given him a hug and congratulated him on giving a really first-rate performance.

And she'd thanked him for doing what he had to do—and what she'd never had the nerve to suggest—in order to get a reaction out of Kelley.

And Buckley had smiled his lopsided smile at her and taken her praise as his due.

And then he'd excused himself and hurried off to change, so he could get to the cast party, where—Julie hadn't the slightest doubt—he expected to pick up with Kelley, exactly where he'd left off with her on stage.

If he hadn't been in such a hurry, Julie might have told him that Kelley was furious with him.

That she considered the liberty he'd taken with her thoroughly unprofessional and totally disgusting.

And that there wasn't a chance in hell she'd come

around to forgiving and forgetting in time for the cast party, so he might as well forget it.

But the way it was at the time, there wouldn't have been any point. As fired up and hot to trot as he was, Buckley wouldn't have heard a word she said.

So here he was now—after the cast party had been going on almost long enough for Julie to eat herself full—wandering over to her table to say hello and resume their conversation.

Except he didn't say hello.

He said, "She isn't coming!"

"Who?" asked Julie—although she knew damned well who Buckley was talking about.

"Kelley!" said Buckley.

Julie shrugged and said, "Her loss."

And then she turned her attention to her *zabaglione*.

"She *hates* me!" said Buckley.

He was getting loud.

Julie looked at him.

"Have you been drinking?" she asked him.

He had. She could tell. His face was flushed and his eyes were glittery.

He raised his voice another notch.

"You know what pisses me off?" he asked her. "I wouldn't have done *any of this*, if it wasn't for *her!*"

People were starting to look now.

Ignoring them and keeping her voice conversational and low, Julie said, "You wouldn't have done it for you?"

Buckley pointed his finger at her and waved it in her face.

His voice rising to a shout, he said, "You took *advantage* of me!"

Her patience wearing thin, Julie said, "Did I?"

"You *knew* I'd want to—"

He didn't want to admit it.

But Julie didn't want to let him deny it.

"You'd want to what?"

"She's *so* beautiful!"

Wallowing in self-pity, Buckley hung his head and shook it.

Julie knew she should let it go at that, but her temper got the best of her.

"Is that all it takes?" she asked.

Buckley glared at her.

"I'm not *talking* to you!" he shouted. "You *used* me!"

He spun around and took off for the door.

Julie called after him, "We used each other!"

But Buckley didn't look back. He just kept walking, straight across the dance floor and out the door.

Everybody's eyes were on Julie.

Taking a deep breath, she turned back to her table.

Lifting her spoon, she muttered, "Bastard!" and stabbed it into the heart of her *zabaglione*.

Slipping into a chair beside her, Patriciana said, "What's wrong with *him?*"

"Where would you like me to begin?" asked Julie.

"Any place you'd like," he said.

"On the way home," Julie answered.

"Pardon?"

"Would you mind?" she asked. Suddenly, she felt old enough to get birthday greetings from Willard Scott. "I've about had it."

Running his eyes over the crowd, Patriciana shook his head and sighed. "Do you think anyone will miss me?"

As they rose from the table, Julie took Patriciana's arm and said, "Poor Bob."

As they moved through the crowd, working their way to the door, Patriciana said, "As difficult as it is to remember sometimes, Short Hills High School is *not* the world."

As they walked out the door and into the bar and saw Buckley—standing at the bar, waving at the bartender, trying to get his attention—Julie said, "Amen to that."

Sixteen

He awakened to the sound of church bells tolling and thought, for a moment, he must be in heaven.

He tried to rise from the bed on which he lay, but the sharp pain that he felt in his side brought him back to earth and reminded him of the grievous wound he'd suffered, fighting at the side of the Rightful King and the Only True Heir to the Throne of Ancient Ireland.

The pain must have caused him to cry out because the next thing he remembered was hearing a voice say, "He lives!"

And then a second voice—so like the voice of an angel, he thought he must be in heaven after all—answered and said, "His fever has broken. Run and tell the King."

"Yes, My Lady."

He heard footsteps departing and then, a moment later, standing over him, he saw her—her that, here on earth, was so like an angel to a sinner such as he.

She smiled down at him.

"My Lord," she said. "We have won the day. Our King is restored to the throne."

"My..."

He tried to speak, to tell her of his joy, but his pain was such that he could not.

"Hush," she told him. "You mustn't speak. You must save your strength. You have had a close brush with death. Until your strength is recovered, you must lie still and keep silent and stay warm. It is the King's command."

But even as she spoke, a sudden gust of wind blew in at the window—flickering the candles and chilling him to the marrow of his bones.

She saw the shivers rake over him and she registered alarm.

Hurrying to the window, she secured it with heavy draperies.

Then, walking about the room, she blew out the candles, one by one.

When the last candle was extinguished, she came to the side of his bed.

There, in the light of the moon, she let her robe slip from her shoulders and fall about her feet.

Lifting his cover, she slipped into the bed beside him.

He felt her beside him, as warm as a summer's day, and said, "Sara Beth! If I'm ever going to get this homework finished, I've got to stop thinking about Sara Beth."

And with that, Sean scrapes his chair back from his desk and heads for the kitchen.

It's Monday night, around nine-thirty. His mother is off at some gallery opening in Noho. His sister, if you believe her, is at her friend Patti's, studying for some big exam.

Sean is wondering why—since he's got the whole apartment to himself—he's been hiding out in his room.

He opens the door to the refrigerator and begins searching through it, looking for something to nibble on.

As he does, he thinks, maybe, he should move his books and papers out into the living room.

That way, he tells himself, at least he can spread out and make himself comfortable, while he sits over his homework and dreams about Sara Beth.

He can't believe how much he wants her!

More than anybody or anything he's ever wanted before!

And he definitely can't believe that he's practically given his word not to feel the way he feels about her!

Or—if he's foolish enough to feel what he feels—not to do anything or even say anything about it!

And he *knows* that just hanging out with Sara Beth—as much as he wants her and as committed as he is to holding up his end of their bargain—has got to drive him bananas!

There's nothing to eat. In the refrigerator. Nothing interesting, anyway.

Closing the refrigerator, Sean tells himself he's got to put an end to this, here and now. Even if it breaks his heart.

There's a telephone mounted on the wall next to the refrigerator. Sean picks it up and dials Sara Beth's number.

As he hears the phone ringing at the other end of the line, he steels himself for what's to come.

He tells himself he's made the right decision, he's doing the right thing.

For himself and for Sara Beth.

And for Jack Ramsey.

Good old Jack.

And then he hears a click as someone lifts the receiver at the other end of the line, and then he hears her voice—so like the voice of an angel that, for a moment, he thinks he must be in heaven after all—saying, "Hello?"

Telling himself, *This is it!,* Sean takes a deep breath and says, "Pizza?"

"No," she says, "Cavanaugh."

"GENNARO'S PIZZERIA" says the sign over the door of the storefront pizza parlor on the east side of Lexington Avenue between Eighty-third Street and Eighty-fourth.

Arriving a moment after Sara Beth, Sean looks across the street and sees her, framed in Gennaro's front window, like a dancer in a spotlight, encircled by the night.

As he stands watching, the counterman approaches Sara Beth and asks if he can help her.

Sara Beth smiles and shakes her head and tells him, no, he can't help her, she's waiting for someone.

Then she turns and glances toward the door—as if the someone she's waiting for might walk in at any second.

Now she looks up and studies the oversize menus, mounted on the walls above the counter.

And while there is nothing unusual in any of these things she does, there is something about Sara Beth—about the particular way she looks, as she whiles away the seconds, waiting for Sean to arrive—that transforms her simple solitude into something mysterious, something enchanting, something timeless.

Now she's looking at the clock, mounted on the wall. She's thinking, *He's late,* and she's getting pissed.

She's pissed! Sean tells himself. *I'm late!*

Pulling himself together, Sean dashes across the avenue, slows to a casual stroll as he hits the sidewalk, and then saunters in through Gennaro's front door.

"Sorry," he says. "Have you been waiting long?"

"No," says Sara Beth. "I just got here."

They order pizza.

Individual slices.

She orders hers with extra cheese.

He orders his with anchovies.

She says she hates anchovies.

He says he won't force her to eat his slice.

"Here or to go?" asks the counterman.

It's a nice night. Warm for this time of the year. There's maybe even a hint of spring in the air.

They order their slices to go.

Sean says it's his turn to pay.

Sara Beth laughs and lets him.

Like carefree vacationers strolling through the exhibits at a theme park, they walk down the avenue, eating pizza and checking out the shop windows.

And it's so great just hanging out with Sara Beth that Sean can't imagine why he'd ever think of giving it up.

After all, what could be bad about spending a springlike

autumn night bopping down Lexington Avenue with a beautiful girl, munching on hot pizza and talking about nothing in particular—just school and football and the stuff in the shop windows and the people that you pass on the street?

"Is that Marcy?"

There's a short brunette in a blue duffle coat trudging down the street toward them and, from where Sean stands, she looks a lot like Sara Beth's friend Marcy Bates.

"Who?" says Sara Beth.

"Mar—"

"God! It is!"

Panicking, Sara Beth clutches Sean's arm and burrows into his side.

Quickly, Sean puts his arm around her and hustles her into the doorway of a closed shoe shop. Steering her to the deepest corner of the doorway, he leans her back against the farthermost shop window, stretches his arms out on either side of her, leans close to her, and shields her from view.

They stand like that—Sean and Sara Beth, face-to-face, looking into each other's eyes—not more than a few inches apart.

Neither of them says a word, at first.

Then, Sean whispers, "Why are we hiding?"

In a whisper, Sara Beth starts to explain.

"Because . . ."

But she can't. Not really.

Her eyes on Sean's, she shakes her head and says, "I don't know."

His eyes on Sara Beth's, Sean says, "We don't have anything to hide, do we?"

Sara Beth shakes her head.

"Not yet," she says.

And then—as if she can't believe what she's said—she smiles and blushes and bites her lip.

And then—although *he* can't believe what she's said—Sean holds his breath and leans ever so slowly forward, until his mouth has found Sara Beth's mouth and Sara Beth's mouth has opened to him.

And at that exact moment, as he closes his eyes and loses himself in Sara Beth's kiss, Sean Manning knows, without a doubt, that he is, for the first time in his life, quite simply, quite totally, quite madly in love.

And when, finally, their kiss is over—and neither of them says a word, but they both look at each other for a long time and then turn to go—Marcy is standing there, staring at them.

Except she isn't Marcy.

In fact, except for the blue duffle coat, she looks nothing at all like Marcy.

Sean looks at Sara Beth and she looks at him and they both crack up.

And then, as they waltz by this girl on their way out the door, Sara Beth tells her, "Good night," and Sean says, "Thanks."

And the girl just looks at them, as they laugh and link their arms around each other's waists and hurry off down the street and turn a corner and disappear from sight.

They kiss again at Sara Beth's front door. Sean kisses Sara Beth.

He doesn't wait for an invitation this time, either. He just takes her in his arms and kisses her. And it's just like the first time.

And when it's over, Sara Beth buries her head in Sean's chest. And Sean holds her in his arms. And neither of them speaks for a second. And for that second East End Avenue seems as silent as a church.

And then, in a whisper, Sara Beth says, "I have to go."

And Sean releases her from his embrace, but—holding on to her hand—he looks into her eyes and says, "Will you go out with me Saturday night?"

She looks at him and shakes her head.

"I don't know," she says.

"I love you," he tells her.

She lowers her eyes.

"I'm going with Jack Ramsey," she says.

"Do you love me?" he asks her.

She shakes her head.

"I don't know," she says. "I have to think."

She raises her eyes to his. There are tears in her eyes, as she says, "Please. Let me. I'll call you. Okay?"

He nods.

"I want you," he tells her.

And he pulls her to him to kiss her once more.

But she holds back and shakes her head and says, "Don't."

And then, bursting into tears, she turns and disappears inside her house.

And Sean stands there for a moment, not knowing where he stands.

And then, shaking his head, he laughs.

And he hops up on the banister that guards Sara Beth's front stairs.

And he slides down the banister to the sidewalk, nearly busting his ass in the process.

And reaching the sidewalk, he fights for his balance and keeps his feet and turns and heads for home.

Seventeen

She heard the doorbell. It was about ten-thirty Wednesday night. It had been a long day and it still wasn't over.

Since right after dinner, she'd been up in her room, trying to memorize all the words that had been added to her French vocabulary in the weeks since she'd agreed to direct *The Philadelphia Story* and stopped paying serious attention.

There was a flood of them—a *déluge*.

It takes a lot of concentration, memorizing one word after another, but up until a minute ago, her concentration had been unwavering, *formidable*.

Then, about a minute ago, as she looked at the next word on her list—*brouillard*—her mind began to fog.

In a flash, she found herself thinking about the review that was scheduled to appear in tomorrow's edition of *The Short Hills Register*.

The show had already been reviewed in *The Blade* on Monday. But *The Blade* was only the school paper. So even though Jon Crowley's review was an unqualified rave for practically everybody and almost everything, it didn't really mean all that much to her.

On the other hand, the review in the *Register*—which, being the only regular weekly newspaper published in Short Hills, was read by practically everybody in town— meant quite a lot.

Of course, she'd heard that some of the most famous directors swore they never read their reviews.

But she wasn't a famous director and she couldn't help hoping that Miles Hanna, the *Register's* drama critic, had been blown away by the show and by the work of its *extremely gifted young director, Ms. Julie Stillwell.*

Ms. Stillwell, she imagined his review might read, *has transformed a handful of youngsters into a company of highly accomplished actors and actresses, fit to take their places beside—or even in front of—the justly celebrated Brat Pack that's currently setting Hollywood on its ear.*

Indeed, when compared to the work of Mike Nichols, Ms. Stillwell's gift for comedy—

That was as far as she'd gotten, reading her fantasy rave review, when the doorbell rang and brought her back to everyday *réalité.*

According to her trusty Casio, it was twenty after ten. She wondered who could be ringing the doorbell at this hour.

She wondered which of her parents would tear themselves away from *St. Elsewhere* and go to the door.

She imagined it would be her father, since her mother was such a diehard *St. Elsewhere* fan.

A moment later, she heard footsteps on her stairway. "Julie?"

Wrong again.

It was her mother.

As much as she hated tearing herself away from her French vocabulary, before her mother had climbed halfway up the stairs Julie was standing at her door.

"The reporter's here," said her mother.

"From the *Register?*" asked Julie.

Her mother laughed.

"From *The Philadelphia Story,*" she said.

Jesus! thought Julie. *What's Buckley doing here?*

After the stunt he'd pulled at the cast party, just the thought of him made her angry.

"I'm not here," she told her mother.

And then, before her mother could respond, she stepped back into her room and closed the door behind her.

She'd seen Buckley at school several times since his outburst, but she'd always avoided him. She had nothing to say to him. Not until he apologized. Not until he walked up to her and said he was sorry for what he'd said at the cast party and the way he'd said it.

Like he meant it! she thought.

Her mother knocked at her door.

"Julie?" she said.

She opened the door and stepped inside the room.

"I'm not here," Julie insisted.

"What's he done?" asked her mother.

Julie had never told her mother about Buckley and the scene he'd made Saturday night at the Villa Bella. Her mother had taken such pleasure in her apparent success, Julie didn't want to do anything to spoil it for her.

So now she said, "What *hasn't* he?"

Taking her evasion in stride, Julie's mother said, "Maybe he's come to apologize."

Julie shook her head and told her mother, "He's not the type."

Her mother smiled as if that was a joke, and said, "Whatever he's done, don't you think you owe him a chance to—?"

"He's *had* a chance!" said Julie.

"He has something for you," her mother said.

That was a surprise.

"What?"

As offhandedly as she could, with a shrug and a smile, her mother said, "It looks like a copy of tomorrow's paper."

How could he! thought Julie. *It doesn't come out until late afternoon!*

"Fresh off the press," said her mother. "But if you want me to tell him you're not—"

"That's okay," she told her mother.

As she took off for the door, she called out to Buckley, "You've got the paper?"

Standing in the entryway at the bottom of the stairs, smiling up at Julie with his village idiot's grin, Buckley said, "Yup."

He looked so pleased with himself, Julie could have spit.

But she was too refined. Hiding her excitement behind a mask of cool indifference—because she didn't want to give Buckley the satisfaction and because, win or lose, the review in the *Register* was only one man's opinion, after all—Julie descended the stairs.

As she reached the landing, Buckley took the newspaper from under his arm, handed it to her, and said, "Peace?"

She wanted to grab the paper out of his hand and read the review.

Indeed, when compared to Mike Nichols, Ms. Julie Stillwell's gift for comedy . . .

But she fought the temptation.

Keeping her hands at her sides, she said, "Have you read it?"

Buckley grinned and nodded.

"Uh-huh," he said. "Congratulations."

"Why don't you offer your friend a chair?" said Julie's mother.

She'd followed Julie down the stairs and paused to play genial hostess on her way back into the living room.

"Oh, yeah," said Julie, acting as if she'd forgotten to be polite when—in fact—she'd intended to be brief.

With barely disguised reluctance, she asked Buckley, "Would you like to come down to the basement?"

"Sure," said Buckley.

She showed him the way.

In the finished basement, when they arrived at the bottom of the stairs, Buckley held the paper out to Julie and said, "Here."

Sounding as cool as she could under the circumstances, Julie said, "Thank you," and took the paper.

It was folded open to the review.

The headline above the review read:

FINE "PHILADELPHIA STORY" AT SHORT HILLS HIGH

Then, beneath Miles Hanna's byline, the review began.

In a highly polished and thoroughly satisfying production, before a standing-room-only crowd at the Short Hills High School auditorium last Saturday night, Philip Barry's classic *The Philadelphia Story* proved itself a timeless beauty, full of comic insights, as delightful and true today as they were when the play was first presented over a half century ago . . .

"All right!" said Julie.
"Yeah," Buckley agreed.
Julie read on.

Playwright Barry has found a true champion in the talented young director Julie Stillwell, whose sense of style and pacing is unerring . . .

"Wow!" said Julie.
"Wait'll you see what he says about me!" said Buckley.

Nor could anyone hope to find a young actress as beautiful and accomplished as the star of the evening, Ms. Kelley Seaver . . .

"Mm," said Julie.
As far as Julie was concerned, aside from her reaction to

Buckley's kiss, Kelley's performance had seemed both un-inspired and uninspiring.

"He wasn't crazy about Kelley," said Buckley with a reassuring smile.

"He wasn't?"

Buckley shook his head.

Indeed, if any fault could be found with the current production, it would have to be with Ms. Seaver's highly accomplished impersonation of the emotionally distant Tracy Lord.

If anything, Ms. Seaver was a little too convincing in her icy detachment from her partners in comedy...

"Damn!" said Julie.

"'However,'" said Buckley.

However, with the assistance of Roy Buckley—a very gifted young man with the panache of a teen-aged James Stewart—

"James Stewart?" said Julie.

"Panache?" said Buckley.

For an instant, Julie flashed on her French vocabulary, sitting on her desk upstairs, waiting to be memorized.

—director Stillwell was able to turn her leading lady's exaggerated coolness to the play's advantage.

Under the sure hand of his director, Mr. Buckley's wonderfully romantic and strikingly real performance served as a challenge to the imperious Ms. Seaver's dominance of the stage.

In fact, at the moment of her astonished surrender to Mr. Buckley's undeniable charms, Ms. Seaver was at her most convincing...

Julie had to laugh at that.

"Jesus!" she said, shaking her head.

"Not bad, huh?" said Buckley. "I'm thinking about becoming an actor."

Turning his profile to Julie, he lifted his chin and looked at her out of the corner of his eye.

"What do you think?" he asked her.

"Looks aren't everything," she told him.

He laughed.

Julie went back to the review, reading it—with its high praise for everyone involved in the production from the Dramatic Society's faculty advisor to the prop man—straight through to the end.

Those who were on hand for the performance were treated to a first-rate evening of theater—the best that has been seen in this vicinity for many a season. Those who were unable to attend really missed something special.

"He liked it!" Julie shouted.

She couldn't contain herself. She threw her arms around Buckley.

It startled the hell out of him.

"Yeah," he said. "We did all right."

Suddenly, remembering who it was she was hugging, Julie disentangled herself and backed away.

"Can I show it to my mother?" she asked.

"Sure," said Buckley. "But—"

"But what?"

"But thanks," said Buckley.

"Thanks?"

He grinned.

"You probably won't believe this," he said, "but I don't get asked to play big handsome guys who sweep girls off their feet all that often."

"I can believe it," Julie told him.

"Not to mention," he said, "all the help you gave me . . ." He shook his head. "Getting me to believe that I was—or could be—that kind of guy . . ."

Julie wished he hadn't brought that up.

Buckley smiled and said, "I guess you can't always count on getting that kind of help. But—"

"Just doing my job," said Julie.

Buckley nodded.

"But you did it so well!" he said.

He laughed and shook his head.

Julie said nothing.

Buckley went on.

"What I said at the party," he told her, "about you using me—I didn't mean it."

The hell you didn't, she told herself.

"I was just—"

Oh, no you don't! she thought.

He shrugged and made a little helpless gesture with his hands.

"Crazy, I guess."

"Not in this court," she told him.

"Hey!" he said. "After the cafeteria, you had me half believing I was as irresistible as Mike Connor! Do you know what that feels like?"

Julie just looked at him.

"It can make you crazy," he told her, "thinking maybe there's hope for you after all."

Don't make me start feeling sorry for you, she thought.

"Thinking maybe 'Lousy with Girls' is just a phase you've been going through for the last seventeen years."

He laughed at that.

Not before I've heard you apologize, she told herself.

"Anyway," he said, "by the time I got to the love scene, I'd pretty much snapped into it, you know?

107

"And for one crucial second there, I actually thought I could sweep Kelley away—not Tracy, *Kelley*—just blow her away with a kiss.

"Can you believe it?" he asked her.

Julie nodded.

"Yes," she said.

What she *couldn't* believe was how *little* Buckley thought of *himself!*

It was like how *much* he thought of *Kelley!*

She couldn't believe *that*, either!

"The whole thing with Kelley," he said. "I've never been that close to anybody who was so . . ."

"Empty?" Julie suggested.

It just jumped out of her.

From where? she wondered.

Buckley looked amazed. Maybe even offended.

"I didn't mean that," Julie told him.

"No," said Buckley. "Maybe she is. Although you couldn't prove it by me. I never got any deeper than how beautiful she was."

"Neither did she," said Julie.

Buckley just looked at her.

"I'm sorry," she said. "I'm not catty. Ever. I swear."

"That's okay," said Buckley. "You're probably right. I've thought about it. The truth is, I know Tracy a lot better than I know Kelley. I don't know Kelley at all.

"What kind of a guy falls in love with a girl he doesn't know at all?" he asked her.

And he looked away.

Because, she imagined, he couldn't stand for her to see how much it hurt and what a fool he felt like.

And watching him, she shook her head and thought, *But he's so funny! And so smart!*

And if she'd never thought he was cute before, at this moment—just standing there in front of her, looking off into space—he was beyond cute.

He was—in his humility and his incredible vulnerability—sexy as hell.

"Appearances aside," he said, "I'm not Mike Connor."

Turning back to look at her, he smiled and said, "As a matter of fact, as of right this minute, the girls that I've actually swept off their feet can be counted on the fingers of one foot."

"Not that it's any of my business," Julie began. *Don't do this!* she warned herself. "But it seems to me," she continued, "if you're out to impress girls—or other people—instead of convincing yourself that you're somebody that you're not—like Mike Connor, for example—you'd be a lot better off just getting good at being whoever you actually happen to be. You know what I mean?

"I mean, Mike Connor isn't even *real*, for Christ's sake!"

What are you getting so mad about? she wondered.

She shrugged and tried to let it go.

"Well," she said, "that's what I think, anyway. Not that anybody asked me.

"I think you have to just go on being yourself, until you run across somebody who's knocked out by who you are.

"Not that it's gotten me anywhere so far," she admitted. "But someday it will. Or else."

"Or else what?" Buckley asked her.

Julie shrugged.

"Or else it won't," she told him.

Buckley smiled at her.

It was a really friendly smile—like you'd give a friend you were really fond of and hoped the best for.

A really nice smile.

"Anyway," said Julie, "if you want me to say I forgive you . . ."

"I do," said Buckley.

Has he apologized? she wondered.

But it was too late to wonder.

109

"I forgive you," said Julie.

"Thanks," said Buckley.

"Do you forgive *me?*" asked Julie.

Buckley didn't understand.

"For helping you believe that you were Mike Connor," she explained.

"Oh," said Buckley. "Sure.

"Hey!" he said. "For as long as it lasted, I loved being Mike Connor!"

No! she thought. *You* still *don't get it*.

But rather than belabor her point, she said, "Because you're a ham. In case you haven't figured that out yet, either."

He hadn't. She could see that. Apparently, up until this very minute, Buckley had never admitted to himself how much he actually craved the crowd's attention.

"Yeah," he said, "I guess you're right."

Admitting it now made him smile.

"And maybe," she said, "because you're a ham and a fairly talented one at that, being an actor isn't such a ridiculous idea."

He looked at her for a second and then broke out laughing.

"I'm serious," she told him.

He saw that she was.

And *she* saw that she had him thinking about it.

"Christ," he said, "an actor! Wouldn't that be weird?"

"Well," she said, "I've got a lot of homework . . . "

He didn't hear her at first. He was off somewhere in his head. Probably signing autographs.

But then after a second, it registered.

"Oh," he said. "Sure."

He started for the stairs, but caught himself and turned back to Julie.

"You can keep the paper," he said. "I got a bunch of them."

"Thanks," said Julie.

"Sure," said Buckley.

And their meeting was over.

They'd never even sat down. They'd just stood there in the basement, at the bottom of the stairs, the whole time.

Now, Julie led Buckley back up the stairs to the front entryway.

As she opened the front door for him, against her better judgment, Julie tried—one last time—to make Buckley see her point.

"I think," she said, "if you'd just try being yourself for a while, you might find somebody who'd appreciate you for who you are."

Buckley stepped out onto the porch.

"Who I am," he said, "is the kind of guy girls come to for laughs. Or to help them out with their homework. I never met a girl who actually wanted to . . ."

He shrugged and looked away.

"Maybe you have," said Julie. "And you just didn't know it."

"What do you mean?" asked Buckley.

Without saying another word, *without thinking another thought,* Julie reached her arms up around Buckley's neck, brought his mouth down to hers and kissed him.

And there it was again!

The feeling she'd felt when she kissed him before.

In the cafeteria at school.

After the dress rehearsal.

When she was pretending she was Tracy Lord and he was pretending he was Mike Connor.

Only this time, there was no pretending.

This melting . . .

This floating . . .

This spinning . . .

So amazing . . .

So exquisite . . .

So perfectly right was ...
Real.
Everything else was ...
Nothing.
There was nothing else but ...

"Buckley..."

Her eyes still closed, Julie rested her cheek against Buckley's chest and nestled, breathless, in his arms.

Amazing! she thought.

"Julie?"

She *loved* the sound of his voice, speaking her name.

"Mm?" she said.

"What was that?"

Jesus! she thought. *What* was *that?*

As if awakening from a dream, she opened her eyes and looked up to see Buckley's funny-sad eyes looking down at her; his sensuous mouth curled in a lopsided grin.

Disentangling herself from his embrace, she said, "How the hell should I know?"

Buckley laughed.

"Good night, Julie," he said.

Smiling to hide the wave of embarrassment she felt sweeping over her, Julie said, "Good night, Buckley."

As Buckley turned and walked down the steps and over to his car, she watched after him and sighed with relief.

She waited while he started up and backed out of the driveway.

She waved to him as he drove off and disappeared from sight.

And then, when he was gone, she let herself back into the house.

"Mom," she called. "They loved it!"

As she closed the door behind her, she thought, *And so did I!*

Eighteen

"Would you do my back?"

He'd walked in on her while she was bathing. She didn't seem to mind.

She smiled and held the soap out to him. Her breasts were—

"Ball!"

As the bodies fly at him from every direction, Sean thinks, *Jesus! Not again!*

"Manning!"

As Sean digs himself out from under the pileup, the coach bellows from the sideline. This is the fourth time today Sean's dropped a snap from center, and the coach is about to deliver a bear cub.

"What do you think you're doing?" he screams.

Sean screams back at him, "Fumbling?"

Webber laughs.

A couple other guys snicker.

"Lazar!" the coach screams.

"Yes, sir!"

Paul Lazar is Sean's backup, a talented junior who almost never gets a chance to work with the first team.

"Get in there!" the coach commands him.

"Manning!" he shouts. "Sit down!"

"Yes, sir," says Sean.

He doesn't give a damn. About practicing today. Or playing tomorrow. Or doing anything else ever, for that matter.

He's blown it with Sara Beth.

Unsnapping his chin guard, he sets out jogging toward the sideline.

It's Friday afternoon and since Monday—when he asked Sara Beth to go out with him Saturday night and she said she'd let him know—he hasn't heard a word from her.

By now he no longer expects to.

He moved too fast. He pushed her too hard.

It's over.

Reaching the sideline, he finds a spot for himself, next to Escabedo and well down the line from the coach.

"She must be something, huh?" says Escabedo.

"What are you talking about?" Sean asks him.

Escabedo smiles, like he sees right through him.

"Your girlfriend," he says.

Sean doesn't smile.

"What are you talking about?" he says.

Escabedo laughs.

"Come on, man," he says. "I got one, too."

Sean turns on him.

Losing control with every word, his voice rising to an angry shout, he says, "What's the matter with you, schmuck? Don't you get it? *I* don't!"

Escabedo just looks at him for a second and then he shrugs and turns his back on him and walks off.

Right away, Sean feels like a shit.

But he's feeling so rotten, in general, that going after Escabedo and telling him he's sorry seems as pointless as everything else.

He can't blame Sara Beth for choosing Jack Ramsey over him.

The truth is, she'd have to be crazy *not* to choose a hundred-percent, certified, all-American winner like Jack over a guy like him, who she only just barely agreed to hang out with in the first place.

And Sara Beth wasn't crazy.

He was.

How could he have imagined—?

Because she let him kiss her?

Christ! he thinks. *Who in the 1980's believes in kisses? Fools,* he tells himself. *Fools like me*.

"Laps!" bellows the coach.

Sean falls into a pack with his teammates and together they begin the fast jog—five times around the field—that ends each day's practice session.

And as he jogs, Sean sees himself fading back to throw a pass.

He sees a huge linebacker busting through the line, shedding blockers and hitting him with the force of a charging rhino.

As he feels his leg twist beneath him and hears it snap, he sees Sara Beth—screaming, as she rises from her seat in the bleachers.

Rising beside her, Jack Ramsey puts his arm around her and comforts her.

In the stands all around them, everyone rises, silently looking down at the field, where the stretcher-bearers are rushing Sean to an ambulance, parked just beyond the end zone.

"Sean!"

Sara Beth cries out and tries to run to him, but Jack catches her and holds her back.

"Let me go!" she cries, and breaking free of his grip, she races down onto the field.

The ambulance is just pulling away as she reaches it.

As she leaps for it, Sean reaches out from the back of the ambulance and catches her hand.

Then, leaning back onto his stretcher, he pulls Sara Beth down to him and—

"Manning!"

Sean's standing by his locker, getting dressed, when the coach bellows his name and calls him to his office.

"Yeah!" he calls back to him.

He finishes zipping up and cinching his belt.

And then, while his teammates steal glances at him and exchange glances with each other, Sean makes his way out of the locker area and down a corridor to the coach's office, acting like he doesn't notice or care.

"Close the door," the coach tells him.

His head bent over his desk as usual, he's pretending he's busy with paperwork as usual and making Sean wait, as usual.

Now, he looks up.

"You got something on your mind out there besides football?"

"*Is* there something else besides football?" Sean asks him.

"No!" the coach shouts and pounds his desk with his ham-size hand. "Not for my starting quarterback, there isn't. Are you my starting quarterback?"

Sean shrugs.

"I guess that's up to you."

"No," says the coach. "It's up to you!

"You walk in here tomorrow with a head full of butterflies and I'll sit your ass on the bench so hard you won't be able to get up off it for the rest of the season.

"What have you got to say to that?"

"I'll try to do better."

"You'd better."

"Is that it?"

"That's it."

As Sean walks out of the coach's office and heads back down the corridor toward the locker area, he sees Escabedo walking up the corridor, heading out.

He doesn't say anything.

And neither does Escabedo.

They just act like they don't know each other as they pass each other by.

But once Escabedo's passed, Sean turns to look after him.

"Hey," he says.

Escabedo stops and turns to him.

"Yeah?" he says.

"I'm going through something," Sean tells him. "It's got nothing to do with you."

"I didn't think it did," says Escabedo. "Anything I can do?"

"Don't rag me about girls for a while."

Escabedo nods and smiles.

"We gonna kick ass tomorrow?" he says.

Sean heaves a sigh.

"Don't we always?" he says.

"Sure," says Escabedo. "We're famous for it. Take it easy, huh?"

And then he turns and walks off.

Except for a few stragglers, mostly guys who stayed behind to get a little extra tape and attention from the trainer, the locker room is almost empty now.

Moving to his locker, Sean picks up his jacket and his books.

Nobody says a word to him as he leaves the locker room.

Walking down the empty basement corridor, it occurs to him that there's no point in his bringing his books home with him tonight. With all he's got on his mind, there's no way he's going to get himself to study.

He decides to drop his books off in his locker, near his homeroom, up on the second floor.

He climbs the stairs to his floor, walks out of the stairwell, turns into the empty corridor, and takes a few steps in the direction of his locker, before he lifts his eyes and sees her—curled up on the floor, leaning back against his locker, reading a book.

"Hi," she says.

"Sara Beth!" he says, smiling so hard he thinks he might crack his cheeks. "What are you doing here?"

"Waiting for you," she says.

He walks over to her and looks down at her.

"But how did you know I'd come up here?" he asks her. "I don't usually."

She smiles and shrugs and says, "It's fate."

"You think so?"

"I've missed you, Sean."

She reaches her hand out to him.

He takes her hand and helps her to her feet.

"You can't imagine," he tells her.

And the next thing he knows, she's in his arms and he's kissing her and she's . . .

You can't imagine.

Nineteen

Julie and Buckley were kissing good night, when Buckley asked Julie if she'd like to drive into New York City on Sunday and spend the day.

It was Thursday night. They'd spent the evening down in Julie's finished basement, studying together, as they had practically every school night ever since last week, when Buckley came calling with his apology and the *Register*'s rave review.

Now, with her parents already upstairs in their bedroom, Julie was at the front door, in Buckley's arms.

Up until now, she'd said yes almost every time Buckley asked her to go anywhere, whether it was going to see a movie, like they'd done last Saturday, or taking a ride over to Paul's Pizza for a slice and a Coke or just riding around in Buckley's car or riding to one of the places that Buckley knew, where there was sure to be no one around.

Even though driving to one of Buckley's secret places usually meant just parking and talking and listening to the radio and fooling around—and even though their fooling around, once it got started, had a way of shifting from sweet to intense with dizzying speed and mind-boggling ease—whenever Buckley had asked Julie to go anywhere, she'd almost always said yes.

But this was different.

Because up until now, whenever Buckley had asked Julie to go anywhere, wherever it was they went, they'd always gone alone.

But that wasn't what Buckley had planned for Sunday.

"I thought making it a double-date might be okay," he told Julie. "If that's okay with you."

It would have been fine with Julie, if the couple that Buckley was thinking about double-dating with wasn't Vicki Hanson and Richie Marra.

But Julie was a little concerned that Vicki and Richie might want to spend the day living up to their reputations.

Julie didn't actually know either Vicki or Richie personally. There were both seniors, who traveled with their own sets.

But with Short Hills being as small as it was and as gossipy as it could be, she knew who they were and she'd heard a lot about both of them.

Vicki was this really pretty girl, who was also supposed to be really smart and really nice.

But she'd spent so much time earning herself a reputation as the hottest girl in town, hardly anybody thought of her as anything else.

Except for Buckley, of course, who thought of her as a kind of oddball—like he was—and, therefore, a kind of friend.

Richie was Vicki's current conquest.

A sometime rock singer and a full-time girlhound, he was almost as handsome as he was vain and, according to the gossip, almost as successful with girls as he claimed to be.

What bothered Julie about double-dating with Vicki and Richie was how the two of them might somehow set the pace for Buckley and her.

Julie wasn't a prude or anything like it, but that didn't mean she wanted to get pressured into trying to keep up with the hottest couple in town, either.

It might have been different if Buckley had turned out to be as inexperienced as she used to think he was.

But he hadn't!

The way it had turned out, Buckley might have been bowled over by Kelley Seaver, but Julie Stillwell was right up his alley.

Still, Julie didn't want Buckley thinking she was afraid to go to New York with him.

So when he said, "How's that sound to you?" she just smiled and said, "This Sunday? Sure. That'd be great."

And it was.

At least, at first.

All the way into New York, Vicki kept talking about all the problems she was having with Sharon.

Sharon—it turned out—was Vicki's mother, but the way Vicki talked about her, it sounded more like she was her wayward daughter.

The problem was, when Vicki's father left her last year, for this airline stewardess he'd met on a flight in from Dallas, Sharon hadn't gone to pieces like any reasonable woman would have.

She'd gone to pieces like an *un*reasonable woman.

Instead of taking her husband's departure as a tragedy, she treated it as an occasion for celebration.

Although she'd been kind of dowdy and proper and even prim all the time that Vicki was growing up, over-night Sharon had turned into a flaming libertine.

She took up smoking, and not just tobacco.

She took up drinking, and not just in the evenings.

And she took up—

With all sorts of men.

Just last week, Vicki had come down to breakfast and found her mother serving Bloody Marys to the man who'd come to fix the dishwasher the day before.

Vicki didn't know what she was going to do about Sharon. She was thinking about sending her off to a good military school, but she was afraid they might break her spirit.

Between laughing along with everybody at Vicki's

"Sharon" stories and joining in with everybody, singing along with the radio, Julie really enjoyed the short drive into the city.

She began thinking she'd been silly to be nervous about making the trip.

The plan was, once they got to New York, they were just going to hang out, check out some clothes stores and record stores in Greenwich Village, maybe wander around Soho, grab something to eat, maybe see a movie—whatever.

That was the plan.

At least, that was the way Buckley told it to Julie.

Except, after they got to New York and parked the car and wandered around the Village for a while, Vicki came up with another plan.

She wanted to "check into a hotel, order up a bottle of Scotch and party until whenever Buckley has to get Cinderella back home from the ball."

Julie thought Vicki was just kidding around.

Until she dragged everybody into a pawnshop on Canal Street and bought a couple of battered old suitcases.

Back out on the sidewalk, she told them, the way she had it figured, if they carried suitcases into the hotel, the desk clerk would think they were regular tourists instead of "just four high school kids out for a friendly little orgy on an autumn afternoon."

As she turned and looked up the street and marched over to the curb, she said, "All we need now is a cab."

"To where?" said Richie.

Lifting the two suitcases, he followed after her.

Julie looked at Buckley.

Buckley smiled and shrugged.

"The Plaza!" said Vicki.

She's actually going to go through with it! thought Julie.

Buckley looked at her.

"You don't want to . . . ?" he asked.

Although Buckley shook his head in anticipation of her answer, it seemed to Julie he was hoping she'd say, "Sure! I'd love to check into a hotel and spend the whole day making passionate love to you. No problem!"

And maybe he was.

But that wasn't what she said.

What she said was, "Get serious!"

Buckley laughed.

"Just checking," he said.

"Check this!" said Julie.

By then, Vicki had flagged down a cab.

"Come on!" she called, as Richie opened the door for her.

Buckley said, "No. Thanks, anyway. We'll just hang out."

Vicki looked at Julie.

Julie felt like she was about twelve.

But Vicki didn't put her down, like she might have. Instead, she smiled like she understood and like, maybe, she was a little envious.

It was at that moment Julie decided that Vicki was really nice and—whatever anybody said—she really liked her.

"Pick us up at seven," said Vicki. "Okay? On the fountain side."

"Good luck," said Buckley.

"See you," said Julie.

And that was that.

Vicki and Richie went off to do their thing, and Julie and Buckley hung out, like they'd planned.

It turned out to be a pretty nice day.

They bought hero sandwiches at an Italian deli in the West Village and then ate them, sitting on a pier, looking out over the Hudson River.

Then they caught a movie. *Mr. Smith Goes to Washington* was playing at Theatre 80 St. Marks.

It was an old movie and Julie had seen it maybe half a

123

dozen times. But she liked it a lot and she thought Buckley ought to see it, at least once, since he'd been walking around for the last couple of weeks thinking he had the "panache of a young James Stewart." She wanted Buckley to see young James Stewart at his panache-est.

If Buckley was really serious about being an actor, like he'd been saying he was, Julie thought he ought to see how far he had to go before he could honestly be compared to a great film actor like James Stewart.

Except the lesson was lost on Buckley because about five minutes into the movie he started kissing Julie and they hadn't come up for air until the movie was over.

As they came out of the theater onto St. Marks Place, Julie asked Buckley what he thought of James Stewart's performance.

Buckley shrugged.

"It wasn't bad," he said. "But it was nothing compared to yours."

Julie felt herself blush.

"We'll have to see it again sometime," she told Buckley.

Buckley broke into a grin.

"Any time!" he said.

Julie gave him a shot in the shoulder, but Buckley just laughed and said, "Okay. Okay. If you can't take a compliment . . ."

By the time Buckley got his car out of the garage where he'd parked it, it was after six-thirty.

Beating their way through heavy traffic, they drove uptown to Fifty-eighth Street and the Plaza Hotel and arrived just in time to pick up the happy couple.

Judging by the smiles on their faces and the way they kind of weaved as they walked to the car, Julie guessed Vicki and Richie had done everything they'd set out to do.

All the way back to Short Hills, they slept in each other's arms.

When they got back to Short Hills—after they'd

dropped Vicki and Richie off at Vicki's house, where Richie had left his car—Buckley and Julie took a ride up to a spot that Buckley knew on an old logging road in the hills behind the high school.

They talked a while, like they usually did. They talked about Vicki and about Richie and about how much fun they'd had in New York.

But they both knew they weren't really talking about anything.

They were just passing a little time before the kissing started.

The kissing was about something.

It was about how much they liked each other and how much they wanted each other.

It was about love and making love.

It was wonderful and wet and urgent.

"Let's go in back."

The backseat of Buckley's Rabbit was about more than kissing.

"Okay."

The backseat was about touching, about hands and breasts and—

"Don't," said Julie. "Please."

"Julie . . ."

His hand was at her waist. His fingers were unfastening her belt.

"I really like you, Buckley."

"Good."

"Don't."

"Why?"

"Because . . ."

"Because why?"

"Because it shouldn't be like this," she told him. "It shouldn't be cramped and rushed and fumbling.

"It should be beautiful. Don't you want it to be beautiful?"

"I just want it to be," he said.

She laughed and kissed him.

"It will," she said. "Maybe. But not now. Okay? Not here."

He heaved a humongous sigh.

"Okay," he said. "You want to go?"

She looked into his eyes and ran her fingers through his hair.

"No," she said. "But let's. Okay?"

"Okay," he said. "Give me a second."

She smiled, as he lifted himself off her and settled into the seat beside her.

It was nice, how much he wanted her.

That he was willing to wait was nicer still.

Twenty

Last night, they'd agreed—instead of Sean picking up Sara Beth at her house this morning—they'd meet at eleven o'clock under the marquee at Loews Orpheum Theater.

Sara Beth was afraid, if Sean kept picking her up at her house every time they went out, sooner or later her parents would start wondering what their daughter and her "new friend" were doing, spending so much time together.

If they ever suspected that their daughter and her "new friend" were doing anything more than just hanging out together, they'd definitely make a huge thing out of it, since they were so protective of Sara Beth and so crazy about—

That was another thing they'd agreed to. Not last night, but right from the first. They wouldn't talk about Jack Ramsey.

Sara Beth said Jack was her problem and talking to Sean about it wasn't likely to help much.

In fact, she said, as torn as she was between what she felt for Jack on the one hand and what she was doing with Sean on the other, even thinking about it hurt quite a lot.

Sean told Sara Beth he understood.

Which he did. And because he did—and because he didn't mind Sara Beth getting into the habit of forgetting about Jack Ramsey as often as she could—he agreed, whenever he and Sara Beth were together, for as long as they were together, they'd both pretend there was no such person as the aforementioned What's-his-name.

It was amazing how good they got at it.

And how fast.

But the fact was, they'd demonstrated a real talent for denying the existence of Whatchamacallit the very first time they had a chance—that Friday, after football practice, when Sean found Sara Beth waiting for him by his locker.

After they kissed, there in the empty hallway, they'd drifted into an empty classroom and gone right on kissing, just as if Whozits never was.

It was the first time they'd let themselves give in to what they felt for each other.

And the way they felt about each other, they might have gone right on kissing forever if—after a while—Sara Beth hadn't thought she heard somebody coming.

Once they stopped long enough to see that no one was coming, they'd realized that somebody might.

And if somebody did, it wouldn't make much sense for them to get caught necking in an empty classroom after school.

So they'd agreed to take a break, thinking it wouldn't last very long and never guessing that it would wind up lasting the whole weekend.

Because that night, after Sean dropped Sara Beth at her door and practically flew all the way home, Sara Beth's parents decided they'd fly up to Boston for the weekend and they'd take their daughter with them—no matter how much she insisted that she'd rather stay at home.

Which meant that Sara Beth missed her chance to see Sean pouring what he had left of his heart and soul into the Dalton game—which Kenyon won, 24–21—and she missed her chance to celebrate the victory with him after the game.

In fact, the way it worked out, Sean and Sara Beth

didn't get around to celebrating late Monday afternoon.

They made a date to meet, the first chan early Monday morning—in the split second it them to pass each other between classes.

Slowing too slightly for anyone to notice, they spoke in voices too low for anyone to hear.

Without wasting the time it would take to say hello, Sean asked Sara Beth if she could meet him somewhere after football practice.

"Yes," said Sara Beth. "Where?"

Sean gave her the name of a backwater luncheonette at the edge of the neighborhood where they wouldn't be likely to run into anybody from school.

They set the time and that was it.

It was four-thirty and already growing dark when Sara Beth walked in the door at the Nueva Amsterdam Café and found Sean sitting in a booth at the back, waiting for her.

They said hello and ordered coffee and then sat for a moment, just looking into each other's eyes.

Neither of them said a word.

One of them couldn't.

Being this close to Sara Beth had triggered Sean's memory of their last encounter and reawakened the incredible desire he'd felt for her when they were kissing.

Propelled by this potent mixture of memory and desire, Sean's brain had rocketed into lunar orbit and left the rest of him sitting there, across from Sara Beth, wide-eyed and speechless.

Fortunately, Sara Beth's silence was entirely voluntary. Otherwise, sitting there the way they were, they were so like statues, they were in danger of drawing pigeons.

But after a while, Sara Beth asked Sean to tell her about the game she'd missed.

She didn't want a summary of who scored when and

ormation. She wanted more

...ate the event for her—as if he
...oing it on the radio—so that she
...ne, play by play, just the way she
...n't been practically forced to go to

...her, Sara Beth's request brought Sean
back... ...rth and broke the spell that had rendered
him spe......

But what was he to say?

He didn't really feel like doing a play-by-play account
of the game. Not here, anyway. And not now.

Even if he left out most of what happened when Dalton
had the ball, it could take forever.

And besides that, it would be embarrassing, trotting out
all the superlatives to describe his own superlative performance.

But on the other hand, he asked himself, now that he
had regained the power of speech, why not?

After all, what was his hurry? Where was he going?

And why should he be embarrassed, if all he was doing
was telling it like it was?

In the end he decided if a play-by-play description of the
game was what Sara Beth wanted, then that's what she'd
get.

It turned out to be a brilliant decision.

Because re-creating the event for Sara Beth gave Sean a
rare opportunity to see her close up, reacting to everything
that happened, just the way she would have if she'd been
sitting in the stands, watching the action unfolding on the
field before her.

And Sara Beth excited—with the color rising in her
cheeks and the fire in her emerald eyes dazzling and flashing—was something to see.

In fact, the sight of Sara Beth excited was so exciting,

there must have been a thousand different times during the time he was telling her about the game that Sean wanted to just lift up and lean across the table and kiss her.

But he restrained himself.

Until he got Sara Beth home.

And then, when neither of them could restrain themselves a second longer, they settled into the shelter of the ivy that framed Sara Beth's front door and kissed until, finally, when they couldn't stand it anymore, they gasped good night and staggered off in opposite directions.

But that wasn't the end of it.

Nowhere near.

All week long, taking advantage of even the slightest opportunity to sneak off and be alone together—even if it was only around a corner and just for a second—they'd gone at it, hot and heavy, every chance they got.

But still, as passionate as they got—as urgently as their bodies pressed together, as desperately as their hands roamed and groped—they never went much further than necking for all they were worth.

Until last night.

They hadn't seen each other after yesterday's game— which Sean and the Crusaders won, beating Hotchkiss 34–20, bringing their season's record to 6–0 and maintaining their position, tied with Hoover, at the top of the league.

Early in the week, Sean's father had agreed to meet with another scout, who'd called to say he was coming up from the University of Miami to see Sean play.

Jay Dunlop was coming from so far away and he was so high on Sean's prospects, Sean's father felt obliged to accept his offer to take Sean and him to dinner after the game.

So it wasn't until after dinner—when he'd thanked Mr. Dunlop and said good night to his father and excused himself from the table at the fancy steakhouse that Mr. Dunlop had taken them to—that Sean finally set out for Sara Beth's.

By then, Sara Beth had already told her parents that Sean was coming over to help her research a paper she was writing about the difference between the lives of teenagers and the way you see the lives of teenagers represented in the media.

Which was why, on his way to Sara Beth's, Sean stopped off at a video rental place and picked up a copy of *Sixteen Candles,* which, somehow or other, Sara Beth had never seen and which, the way it turned out, she didn't like all that much anyway.

They watched the movie on the VCR in Sara Beth's den, and—all through the first half of it, at least—they managed to behave themselves like a couple of right-thinking young adults.

They kept their hands to themselves and their eyes on the TV screen and their minds on the changes that Molly Ringwald was going through.

At least Sean did.

Sara Beth was having a hard time relating to Molly Ringwald, and after a while, when she got tired of trying, she asked Sean if he was ever going to tell her how his dinner with the scout from Miami had gone.

"Sure," said Sean.

He hadn't meant to keep it from her.

So he told her it had gone okay, the steak was good, the scout seemed like a nice enough guy, and, he guessed, if he was going to go to college, Miami might be as good a place as anywhere else.

Which got a laugh out of Sara Beth.

Which surprised Sean.

Sara Beth said she was sorry, but Sean was kidding, wasn't he?

The University of Miami might be many things, she

said, but it definitely was not in a league with the really first-class schools where the really first-class people went.

It wasn't Yale, she said, or Harvard or Notre Dame.

Or Michigan, thought Sean.

"It's *Miami!*" said Sara Beth, as if its second-class status was so obvious that anybody with half a brain could see it.

Sean was so startled by Sara Beth's attitude—*It's got to be something she picked up from Whosee-whatzits,* he thought—that he was about to lie to her and tell her he was only kidding about Miami being as good a school as any. But just then, he happened to notice that Sara Beth's mother was standing at the door.

She and Sara Beth's father had spent the night lurking around the living room, just down the hall. But now, she'd come to say good night.

Which she did. She said good night.

And Sara Beth said good night.

And Sean said good night.

And Sara Beth's mother said good night again.

And then she and Sara Beth's father headed upstairs to bed.

At which point—*forget it!*—Sean and Sara Beth were in each other's arms before her parents were halfway up the stairs.

They'd been sitting on this big old leather couch up until then, but after a second, they weren't sitting anymore.

And while their explorations of one another had never gone beyond the surface up until then, now they found that surfaces were no longer adequate to their needs.

In fact, before they were through, Sean and Sara Beth had gotten about as familiar with one another as they could get without anybody actually removing anybody's clothing.

But finally, long after *Sixteen Candles* had come to an end, Sara Beth said enough.

It was late, she said, and time for Sean to go.

And so he went.

But not before he and Sara Beth had spent another ten or fifteen minutes saying good night at Sara Beth's front door.

It wasn't yet one A.M. when Sean hit the street. He felt like walking. It wasn't such a bad night for November.

Not bad at all, he told himself.

But walking through the park at this hour was asking for trouble, so he decided he'd head down to Central Park South and walk around the park.

It was a lot longer that way and it would take a lot more time, but that was okay. He needed time to think.

Something was bothering him and he couldn't figure out what it was.

It wasn't the thing with Miami, even though it was weird the way Sara Beth had jumped on him for that.

Obviously, as far as she was concerned, when it came to making plans for the future, there was only one way to go—the "really first-class" way—and one place to get to—the top.

He couldn't deny that he'd been kind of thrown by Sara Beth's reaction.

But he was happy that his future meant so much to her.

And he had to admit, when it came right down to it, he wasn't so sure that what she had to say was wrong.

So, it wasn't the thing with Miami that was bothering him.

But something was.

Because he wasn't jumping up and down and counting his blessings and praising the Lord.

Which he ought to be.

Because the most desirable woman in the whole world seemed to think that he was the most desirable man in the whole world.

Or, at the very least, the next thing to it.

And although it was hard to believe—even for an occa-

134

sionally swellheaded hotshot like him—it seemed like Sara Beth Cavanaugh couldn't get enough of him!

And since he couldn't get enough of her either, what more could a guy ask for?

Especially when you considered the odds on such an unlikely situation ever coming to pass.

So why wasn't he jumping up and down, etc.?

Because—

That's all we ever do!

He was halfway home before he realized it.

The whole thing between them was sex.

All the time they spent together, if they weren't actually all over each other, they were either looking for someplace to go where they could be all over each other or they were sneaking back from someplace where they'd been all over each other.

It was as if that was all they had on their minds.

Which was close to true.

At least in Sean's case.

Although he did sometimes think about where their being all over each other might lead.

He thought about that—imagined it, actually—quite often.

Actually.

Particularly in bed at night, before he fell asleep. But the thing was, as astonishing as all the kissing and touching was, it still left Sean wanting more.

Not more kissing and touching or even more physical intimacy. Although he wanted that, too.

But more of Sara Beth.

The way he felt about Sara Beth, if he didn't love her and want to make love to her, he'd still give anything just to get to know her, just to spend some easy time with her and share some ordinary pleasures with her.

But somehow they never seemed to have enough time

for much of that. It seemed as if their chance to form a real friendship was withering away in the heat of their desire.

Sean was afraid, if they just kept on the way they were going, by the time they got around to making love, they'd be perfect strangers.

But he wasn't about to let that happen.

By the time he arrived home early this morning, he'd decided to cut way back on all the kissing and touching.

In fact, before he went to bed last night, he'd made himself a promise.

He and Sara Beth were going to spend this afternoon— Sunday afternoon—together. And Sean promised himself, before he went to bed last night, no matter how great the temptation, he would get through the whole day without kissing Sara Beth even once, without ever taking her in his arms, without even so much as touching her.

Except for maybe just holding her hand in a friendly way every now and then.

Only now, as he stands under the marquee at Loew's Orpheum Theater and sees Sara Beth striding down the street, coming to meet him, Sean feels an incredible pang of regret.

Reminded how beautiful Sara Beth is, he wonders why on earth he ever made such a stupid promise and how on earth he'll ever get himself to keep it.

From half a block away, in her black leather jacket, her skin-tight Western jeans and boots, Sara Beth looks about nine feet tall.

But magically, by the time she's reached Sean and come to a stop directly in front of him—and so close to him that he can almost feel her pressing against him—she's exactly his height or maybe half an inch shorter.

Just right, he tells himself.

"Sean Manning Fan Club reporting for duty," says Sara Beth.

Looking over her shoulder, as if he expected to see a

large crowd trailing behind her, Sean says, "Is this all of you?"

"We're a very exclusive club," Sara Beth explains.

"I see," says Sean. "Then I guess there wouldn't be any point in a chump like me applying for membership."

"Between you and me?" asks Sara Beth.

Sean nods.

"You'd be wasting your time," Sara Beth tells him.

Sean laughs and then, without thinking about it, he reaches out to take Sara Beth in his arms, catches himself at the last second, throws his arms wide enough to encompass the whole city, and says, "Where to?"

"Wither thou goest," says Sara Beth.

"Oo!" says Sean. "Literary!"

"Biblical," says Sara Beth, correcting him.

"Are you suggesting the Bible isn't literature?" he asks her.

"Heaven forbid!" says Sara Beth.

And they both laugh.

And Sara Beth takes Sean's arm.

Whoops! thinks Sean.

But he can't help smiling and feeling a certain sense of relief, as he realizes that Sara Beth isn't bound by the terms of his vow.

"Where to?" says Sara Beth.

Since the plan was just to get together and hang out, Sean has no plans, except maybe—

"It's too nice a day to spend cooped up in dark theater, watching a wonderful old black-and-white movie, right?"

"Have you got one in mind?" asks Sara Beth.

"Kind of," says Sean.

Going through the paper this morning, he happened to notice that *Mr. Smith Goes to Washington* was playing at the Theatre 80 St. Marks.

"It's too nice a day," says Sara Beth.

"Yes," says Sean. "I thought so."

"And anyway," says Sara Beth, "I don't usually like old black-and-white movies."

"Your only flaw as a human being," Sean tells her.

She shrugs.

"It's always something!" she says. "So, where to?"

Like a frontier scout in a John Ford Western, Sean lifts up from his saddle, looks around, gets his bearings, sinks back down in his saddle, nods south, and says, "That way!"

Smiling, Sara Beth takes Sean's hand and together they set out walking southward.

They aren't planning, either of them, to walk as far as Greenwich Village, which is about ten miles south of Loews Orpheum Theater. But it's such a nice day. And once they start walking, there doesn't seem to be any good reason to stop.

The rhythm of their walking and the easy conversation it generates—like lyrics floating on top of a tune—turn the simple act of getting from here to there into something like a dance.

Nonetheless, about an hour later and nearly ten miles away, Sean and Sara Beth have both worked up more than enough appetite to polish off the hero sandwiches that they buy from an Italian deli that they discover in the West Village, not far from the piers that overlook the Hudson River.

And then, when lunch is over, sitting at the end of one of the piers around Christopher Street, feeling fat and happy, Sean looks over at the beautiful young woman sitting beside him.

Her feet dangling and swinging over the edge of the pier, Sara Beth is looking down into the depths of the river, but her thoughts are a million miles away.

In contrast to the sunlight playing on the water behind her, her expression is dark and serious.

And yet to Sean, she is no less beautiful in this somber

mood than she is when her mood is bright and shining—no less beautiful and no less desirable.

At this moment, he'd give anything if he could just put his arm around her and hug her to him and look over at her and catch her looking over at him and smile at her and see her—as he leans to kiss her—smiling back at him.

But up until now, Sean has stuck to the promise he made himself, and so far, he and Sara Beth have been having a good time together, just hanging out.

Which is exactly what Sean hoped would happen when he made his promise to himself.

So, he reasons, if he were to break his promise to himself now, after he's gotten what he hoped for, not only would he feel like he couldn't keep a promise that he made to himself, but he'd also feel like he was being ungrateful for his good luck.

So he reminds himself that tomorrow is another day and he makes up his mind to stick by his promise, straight through to the end.

"Soho?" he says.

Sara Beth turns to him.

"Check out the galleries?" he says. "See what the painters are finding to paint these days? See what the smart gallery-goers are finding to wear?"

In a flash, Sara Beth is back from the land of clouds and shadows.

She's smiling and then she's on her feet and she's reaching down to give Sean a hand.

As he smiles and takes her hand and gets to his feet, Sean wonders what was troubling Sara Beth. It occurs to him that he might ask her. But he decides not to.

If it's important, he tells himself, *she'll tell me in her own good time*.

They set out for Soho.

About a dozen blocks and fifteen galleries later, Sean is standing in the Hankin Gallery on Lafayette Street, trying to concentrate on the paintings and sculpture in their current group show.

But nothing that he sees compares with the sight of Sara Beth—moving among the canvases and constructions, mingling with the crowd.

"Now *that,*" he tells himself, "is art!"

"What are you doing?"

Sara Beth has caught him studying her.

"Taking your picture," he tells her.

"With what?"

"My mind's eye."

"Do you always do that?"

"No," says Sean. "Sometimes I take it with a camera."

She doesn't believe him.

"You do?"

"I did," he tells her. "Once."

"When?"

"Thursday afternoon."

She shakes her head.

"We went for ice cream, Thursday afternoon."

"And I was late," he reminds her.

"Yes," she remembers. "A little."

"Except I *wasn't* late," he tells her. "I got to Emil's before you did.

"But I waited across the street," he continues, "with my camera and my handy telephoto lens. And I got a bunch of shots of you—coming down the street, walking into Emil's, looking around for me, not seeing me, checking out the juke box, the big guy with the red hair . . ."

"I wasn't checking him out!"

"I've got proof!"

"Sure you do."

"Want to see?"

"Yes."

"Come on."

He takes her hand and starts for the door.

"Wait a minute."

She stops him.

"Where are we going?"

"My house."

She smiles at him, like she knows what's on his mind.

"Uh-uh," she says.

Sean laughs.

"My mother's home," he tells her. "And my sister. And probably a half dozen of her friends."

"Are you sure?" asks Sara Beth.

"Do I look like the kind of guy who would lure an innocent girl up to his love nest in broad daylight?"

"Yes," says Sara Beth.

But nonetheless, given Sean's assurances, she goes.

When they arrive at Sean's apartment, there are two notes waiting on the table just inside the front door.

Sean's mother has gone to visit a friend and won't be home until after dinner. There's chicken in the fridge and pizza in the freezer and ten dollars in the sugar bowl.

Sean's sister has gone to her friend Patti's and taken the chicken that used to be in the fridge with her.

"I'd better go," says Sara Beth.

"Why?" asks Sean.

His mind is racing a mile a minute, considering the immediate possibilities, reconsidering last night's vow, weighing one consideration against the other.

"I've been a perfect gentleman all day," he says. "Haven't I?"

"Yes," says Sara Beth, as if it had just dawned on her and she can't believe it. "How come?"

Sean shrugs.

"Just for a change," he says.

Sara Beth smiles.

"Have I been going too fast for you?" she teases.

She moves closer to him.

"I've tried to be gentle," she says.

She lifts her hand to his cheek.

"But you're such a hunk!"

And she kisses him.

And he kisses her back.

But after a second, she pulls away from him.

"Wait a minute!" she says. "This is working out just like you planned it, isn't it?"

Sean laughs.

"No," he says. "It isn't. I just wanted to show you the pictures. So help me!"

But she doesn't believe him.

So Sean sighs and he takes her hand and he looks into Sara Beth's eyes and he says, "You know I love you."

Sara Beth nods.

"But do you know I like you, too?"

"Sean . . . !"

"I don't know you as well as I want to yet," he tells her. "Nowhere near. And you don't really know me, yet.

"I want us to be close," he says. "Like best friends. Don't you?"

Sara Beth doesn't say anything.

For a second, she just stands there, looking into Sean's eyes.

There's something in her expression that reminds Sean of the way she looked when they were back at the pier and she was looking down into the water and drifting off in space.

And then, after a moment, she says, "*Are* there any pictures?"

Sean smiles.

"Do I look like the kind of guy who—"

"Yes," she tells him.

"Right this way," he says.

And taking her hand, he leads her across the living room to his bedroom door.

Stopping at the door, he says, "I'll wait here."

She looks at him and nods.

"Where are they?" she asks.

"You can't miss them," he tells her.

He reaches into his room and switches on the light.

The wall at the far end of the room is floodlit and covered with cork.

Pinned up on it—arranged and lighted like a photo exhibition in a gallery—are more than a dozen different photographs of Sara Beth.

Shot in moody black-and-white, blown up and printed on matte-finished paper, the photographs range from extreme close-ups that hint at smoky secrets deep in Sara Beth's eyes, to full-figure action shots that capture her coltish verve and thoroughbred style.

Standing in the doorway, Sara Beth can't believe what she sees. She glances over at Sean, and then, like a sleepwalker, she steps inside his room.

Sean watches from the doorway as Sara Beth walks to the center of the room, stops and stands, running her eyes over the collection, shifting her attention from one shot to the next.

From where he's standing, Sean can't see the expression on Sara Beth's face or guess at her reaction.

But after a while she begins moving forward, moving in on the photographs, moving slowly and carefully, almost as if she were stalking them.

And while Sean watches her and waits for her reaction, it occurs to him for the very first time that Sara Beth could be really pissed at him for sneaking pictures of her without asking her permission.

Or, even worse, even if she doesn't mind his having taken her picture, she might hate the pictures he took.

When he thinks about it now, the pictures aren't very glamorous. They weren't supposed to be. They were just supposed to be true.

But not everybody prefers true to glamorous. And maybe Sara Beth is one of those who doesn't.

The thing is, there's no way of telling, one way or the other, from where Sean is standing.

But finally, just when he thinks he can't wait another second to hear what Sara Beth thinks, she says, "Wow."

Just like that.

Not loud or excited.

She just says it.

"Wow."

Like that.

Sean says, "Wow?"

And he steps inside his room.

"I really look . . ."

She can't find the word.

Sean moves in beside her and follows her gaze to his favorite shot of her.

"Beautiful," he says.

Sara Beth shakes her head.

"No," she says. "Well, yes. If you mean the photographs. I guess they are. But I've never seen myself this way. Is this how I look?"

"To me," Sean tells her.

"I look so . . ."

"What?"

"I don't know," she says. "Kind of earthy. And real. But not hard. Soft. But strong."

"Yeah," says Sean. "That's about it. And funny."

Sara Beth turns to him then.

There are tears in her eyes.

And now, as a single tear spills over and runs, glistening, down her cheek, Sean says, "Sometimes, anyway."

And he takes her in his arms.

And he kisses her.

And this time, unlike all the times before, there is no rush in their kiss and no desperation.

There is, instead, an exquisite tenderness in the way their lips meet and melt together.

And there is a grace in the way they settle onto Sean's bed.

In the way that Sara Beth guides Sean's hand to her breast.

In the way that Sean—

And then, Sean hears the click of his front door opening.

He hears giggling.

And then he hears his sister's voice calling, "Mom?"

Twenty-one

She wasn't exactly surprised.

When Julie came out of the ladies' room at Mikey's Lounge, she'd expected to find Buckley where she'd left him, sitting at the tiny table between the packed bar and the crowded dance floor. But when she saw he wasn't there, it didn't really surprise her.

She tried to tell herself that he'd probably just gone off to the men's room. But she knew, if she looked, she'd find him out on the dance floor, dancing with Debra Stone.

Debra Stone was one of those girls Buckley sometimes buddied around with. She was probably the cutest of the bunch, if you happen to like willowy brunettes with big black eyes and flat chests and no fannies.

But from the way Debra practically gaped at Buckley when they'd first come in—and the way she'd been sneaking peeks at him ever since—Julie could see that she'd come up with a whole new attitude toward her old pal.

Suddenly, she seemed less interested in being Buckley's buddy than she was in getting her mitts on Buckley's body.

The only question in Julie's mind was just how Debra had managed to achieve her goal so quickly. Her trip to the ladies' room hadn't taken more than minute.

As she ran her eyes over the dance floor, jam-packed with the usual Friday night crowd, Julie wondered how Debra had managed to shake loose of Howie "The Hulk" Hogeboom, the unlimited class wrestler she was with.

When she saw that Julie's back was turned and decided

to make her grab for Buckley, just where did Debra tell Howie she was going?

That's what Julie was wondering when she spotted them, just where she thought she would—out on the dance floor, bopping around and having what appeared to be a real swell time together.

The odd thing was, up until that moment, Julie had been kind of ticked at Debra for abducting her date. But now that she saw Buckley, she realized that she couldn't really blame her. If she'd been in Debra's place, she probably would have taken a shot at Buckley herself. He looked that sharp.

Partly, it was the oversize sport coat he was wearing and the pegged pants and the pointy-collared shirt.

But mostly, it was his semipunk haircut—which was crewcut on the sides and long at the top and featured a wave of curly hair that slashed down across his forehead.

That was the sweetest thing.

The way if had come about.

Tuesday, after school, Buckley had suggested to Julie that she should "try something" with her hair.

At the time, he was driving her over to the mall, where she planned on getting her hair washed and cut and shaped in her usual not-much-to-look-at-but-easy-to-manage way.

But taking Buckley's suggestion to heart, Julie had thrown caution to the wind and wound up with a frizzy permanent that made her look like she'd stuck her finger in a lightbulb socket.

It was pretty shocking. To say the least.

When she came out of the unisex hair salon where she'd had it done, Buckley was waiting for her.

And when he saw what she'd done and said that he loved it—but obviously didn't. Because who could?—Julie burst into tears.

At that moment, the way she felt, she thought she might

as well get all of her hair shaved off and—while she was at it—take holy vows and hide her head under a habit.

Buckley tried to tell her it wasn't that bad and it just took a little getting used to.

But looking at herself in his rearview mirror, Julie could see that she looked like a poster girl for Brillo pads.

She told Buckley to take her home, straight home, with no stopping off on the way.

The truth was, she was mad at him. For making her do it. For making her get the perm. For making her look ridiculous.

Which, she was certain, she did.

The fact that Buckley had only suggested that she "try something" with her hair—and had never mentioned a perm or anything else—Julie completely forgot.

She was devastated. And so far as she was concerned, one way or another, Buckley was to blame.

Once she got home, she raced upstairs to her bathroom, jumped out of her clothes, and hopped into the shower.

She was determined to wash the permanent out of her hair—to shampoo it and condition it and blow it dry, until it came to its senses and straightened out.

It didn't work, of course.

Wednesday morning, when she looked at herself in her bathroom mirror, she started crying, all over again.

When it came time to leave for school, she told her mother she wasn't going—not until her permanent grew out. Until then, she told her, they could pretend she had pneumonia.

She might even have it, she told her mother. Now that she thought about it, she *did* feel kind of feverish.

But her mother—who thought she looked "kind of raffish" with her "new do"—wouldn't go along.

And anyway, she told Julie, Buckley was already parked outside in the driveway, waiting to drive her to school.

She couldn't imagine Julie would want to stand him up.

"Oh, yes I would!" Julie told her. "I'd like to stand him up in front of a firing squad!"

With that, she grabbed her books, stormed out the door, and charged across the driveway to Buckley's car—keeping her head down and her eyes on the ground the whole way; hoping that, somehow, if she didn't look at Buckley, Buckley wouldn't be able to see her.

She didn't look up until she was in the car and sitting next to him.

That was when she finally looked over at Buckley and saw what he'd done to *his* hair.

It was such a shock—*He's got ears!* she thought—that she broke out laughing.

She knew it was rude. But she couldn't help herself.

"Feel better now?" Buckley asked her.

He'd done it for her! Buckley had gone "new wave," just for her!

Like Samson did for Delilah, she thought, *after she got her perm!*

As Buckley started up the car and they set out for school, he told Julie how—after he dropped her off the day before—he'd driven back to the mall and gone into the same unisex barbershop where she'd gotten herself frizzed and got himself chopped.

"Why should you be the only person at school with a weird new haircut?" he asked her. As if he were jealous of all the attention she was bound to get, if he didn't horn in on it.

Which was such a bizarre idea, Julie had to laugh.

Finally.

After all, it *was* pretty silly—the whole thing with her hair.

Even if it *did* look weird. So what?

It wasn't like it was forever.

They only *called* it a permanent. It was actually just a temporary.

In a few months, it would grow out and be gone without a trace.

That's what Buckley was trying to tell her by getting his hair cut.

And that's what—thanks to Buckley—Julie finally realized.

It was the sweetest thing.

The new clothes that went with Buckley's new haircut came the next day.

Buckley said he'd bought them to show the guys who kidded him about his haircut that he couldn't be kidded out of looking any way he wanted to.

But Julie noticed—once he started dressing like a Euro-rocker—the girls at school started looking at Buckley a little differently than they had before.

They started *looking* at him.

Like Debra Stone had.

In a way, Julie didn't mind.

But in another way—

She looked around the bar room, searching for Howie Hogeboom. As huge as he was, he wasn't hard to spot.

Julie didn't know Howie all that well. But since their respective dates were dancing with one another, she felt they had enough in common to start up a conversation.

She wandered over to Howie's corner of the bar and said hello.

Howie didn't seem to recognize who she was at first. But when she nodded toward Debra and Buckley and said, "How did that happen?" Howie managed to put two and two together.

"I don't know," he said. "He walked over and asked me if I'd mind him dancing with Deb."

"He asked *her?*"

"He asked *me*," Howie told her. "And before I could say, 'Yes, I mind,' she said, 'No, he doesn't mind,' and there they are."

Julie followed his gaze to the dance floor, where they certainly were and where they certainly seemed to be having a fine old time.

"Did you do something to your hair?" Howie asked.

"Want to dance?" she replied.

Howie couldn't have looked more surprised if she'd asked him if he wanted to go to bed with her.

"Come on," she said.

Taking his hand, she led him out onto the dance floor.

Twenty-two

If you want her
And she wants you.
No one ever is to blame . . .

They were dancing.

The music poured out of Sara Beth's den and flowed down the hallway and washed over them where they danced, under a crystal chandelier in the entryway at the bottom of the stairs.

At first, they danced back and forth before the huge mirror that presided over the entryway.

But after a while their movement slowed, until they were no longer dancing, but just standing in one place, wrapped in each other's arms, swaying to the music.

Sean was thinking how good it felt and how right, when he felt something tickling his cheek.

Opening his eyes, he leaned his cheek away from Sara Beth's and saw—to his amazement—that Sara Beth was crying.

"What's wrong?"

She just looked at him for a second and then she said, "Don't you know?"

From the way she said it, Sean guessed he ought to, since Sara Beth seemed to think he was to blame for whatever it was that was making her cry.

But he didn't have a clue.

"No," he told her.

She shook her head.

"What's wrong," she sobbed, "is how much I want you!"

Throwing herself against him, she buried her face in his chest and unleashed a torrent of sobs, one more heartrending than the next.

Sean felt happier than he'd ever felt in his whole life.

Sara Beth's bed was a four-poster, as wide as it was long. The sheets, edged with lace, were icy cool against Sean's skin. Sara Beth's skin against his was electric.

He'd made love before. Or at least he thought he had.

But he'd never made love to someone that he loved before, and now that he had, he realized that he'd never made love before.

And now it's over and he's lying there and Sara Beth is lying next to him and he's feeling better than anybody has a right to feel, when suddenly, from out of nowhere, he flashes on Jack Ramsey.

He'd rather he hadn't, of course. But the truth is, as good a guy as Jack is, Sean feels a little bad about stealing his girl.

It's a sincere feeling. But since, at the same time, he also feels pretty terrific about stealing Jack's girl, it doesn't last for more than an instant.

"Sara Beth?"

"Mmm."

She is turned away from him. He kisses the back of her neck.

"Mmm."

"I love you."

He runs the tips of his fingers along her shoulder and down her side and brings his hand to rest at her narrow waist.

She turns and looks over her shoulder at him.

"I love you, too," she says.

153

She rolls over and leans her head down and kisses his nipple.

Then, looking up at him, she smiles and says, "You must think I'm an awful slut."

"No," he tells her. "I think you're a wonderful slut."

She laughs and he reaches down and lifts her up on top of him.

So beautiful, he tells himself.

And, he tells himself, as he brings her mouth to his, *so incredibly mine!*

Twenty-three

"Please," he said.

"No," she told him, gently but firmly.

It was Saturday night. They'd been invited to a party at Vicki's.

"And," she said, "would you kindly remove your hand from . . . Thank you."

They'd gotten as far as Vicki's driveway.

"Are you ready?" she asked him.

They'd been sitting in Buckley's car, necking and fooling around for the past twenty minutes.

"Are you kidding?"

Julie laughed.

"Come on," she said.

She piled out of the car and began weaving her way through the maze of parked cars that clogged the circular driveway that led up to Vicki's front door.

There was no way Vicki could have heard Julie ringing her doorbell over the din of the music that came pounding through her door. There was no way she could have heard Buckley banging the brass door knocker, either.

But somehow she must have gotten the message that someone had arrived on her doorstep, because—just as they were about to let themselves in—Vicki opened the door and saved them the trouble.

"We can't get rid of Sharon," she said, by way of a greeting. "She's having too much fun."

Turning to Julie, she said, "You've never met Sharon, have you?"

"No," said Julie.

"Come on," said Vicki. "I'll introduce you. Maybe you can think of a way to bum her out."

Taking Julie's hand, Vicki led her and Buckley through the crowd gathered in her palatial front hallway with its elegant winding stairway, and into a living room bigger than any living room Julie had ever set foot in before.

There was a fire roaring in the great fireplace at the center of the room, throwing light and shadow over a crowd of kids who were dancing and talking and eating and drinking and leaping and sprawling all over the place.

Among them, gyrating in the flickering firelight at the center of the room, Vicki spotted her mother.

Sharon, as Vicki called her, was doing the Lindy with Paul Giles, who'd been the star linebacker on the football team last year, until he tore up his knee in the game against Union.

Sharon wasn't young anymore, but she was still good-looking and she had a look in her eye that a man might easily take for a willingness to meet him halfway. Especially if the man was a boy like Paul Giles.

The joke about Paul Giles was, even though he couldn't run anymore, he was still just as fast as he'd always been.

In fact, watching Paul dancing with Sharon, seeing the way he was looking at her and she was looking back at him, Julie had the uneasy feeling that Paul was seriously thinking about adding Vicki's mother to his list of conquests.

It wasn't any of Julie's business, of course, but the idea of Paul and Sharon—just thinking about it—gave her the creeps.

"She's a great dancer," she told Vicki.

"It's in her blood," said Vicki. "Along with a judgment-impairing level of alcohol. Beaujolais, last I noticed."

When the music finally stopped—when John Mellen-kamp finally figured out how to spend his "Lonely Old Night," and Paul Giles looked like he might have figured out how to spend his—Vicki brought Julie over to meet her mother.

"Julie Stillwell," she said, "this is Sharon, who is old enough to be my mother, but not necessarily old enough to act like she is."

"Am I being naughty?" Sharon asked her daughter.

"Is the Amazon a river?" Vicki replied.

"How do you do, Julie," said Sharon. "I was just about to put myself to bed."

"Not yet!" Paul Giles protested. "The night's still young."

"So are you, my dear," said Sharon.

Paul Giles looked like somebody had just stepped on his pet frog.

"Nice to have met you, Julie," said Sharon. "And—"

She looked at Buckley.

"Buckley!" she said. "Is that you?"

"Afraid so," said Buckley, smiling shyly.

"Poor thing," said Sharon. "Did it hurt much?"

"Mother!" said Vicki.

But Buckley laughed.

"Naughty again!" said Sharon. "Well, that does it, I'm sure you'll be happy to hear.

"Good night, dear," she told her daughter.

With a wave of her hand, she turned and walked to the French doors at the back of the room, stepped out onto the patio, and moved off toward the pool house, where she'd promised Vicki she'd spend the night.

The moment she was gone, Vicki walked over to her tape deck and ejected John Mellenkamp in mid-song.

"The smoking lamp is lit," she announced. "The bar is open, and—if any of you should happen to find yourselves in any of the rooms upstairs, just be sure you leave them approximately the way you found them, okay?

"Okay," she concluded. "Did somebody say 'Let's party'?"

Somebody shouted, "Let's party!"

Then everybody did.

Vicki popped *Disraeli Gears* into her tape deck and cranked up the volume on "Strange Brew" to dance-club level.

All around the room, people started lighting up joints and passing them around.

A crowd stormed the bar.

One or two couples started edging toward the door and the front hallway, where the elegant winding staircase led up to the rooms on the second floor.

Buckley looked at Julie.

"Let's party," he said.

"Is there a Ping-Pong table?" she asked him.

"Don't you want to dance?"

"I'm the world's best Ping-Pong player," she said.

Not because she was. She was pretty good. But she didn't like what was going on around her and she knew that Buckley was too competitive to let her get away with claiming the world championship.

"It's downstairs," he said.

"Best out of three," said Julie.

"For the world championship," said Buckley.

He showed her the way downstairs to the game room.

The room—the whole downstairs—was empty.

Except for the steady thump of the bass, reverberating through the walls and reminding her of the party that was going on above, Julie might have imagined that she and Buckley had the whole house to themselves.

They warmed up. When Buckley saw that Julie wasn't going to be the pushover he'd imagined, he took off his jacket and rolled up his sleeves and got down to business.

He was good. He was fast and he was flashy. But he had no patience. He slammed everything and, about half the time, his shots sailed clear off the table.

Playing defensively and using lots of backspin—a trick she'd learned at camp the summer before last—Julie won two of the first three games.

And then, when Buckley suggested they make it the best out of five, she won a third.

So they made it the best of seven and then the best out of nine until, finally, after they'd played twenty games, the battle for the world championship was tied at ten games apiece.

By then, both Julie and Buckley were so involved in the contest, they'd pretty much forgotten about the party going on upstairs and the parties going on in the rooms on the floor above that.

Which was fine with Julie.

Nonetheless, when Buckley suggested that they make *this* final game their *final* final game and not just *another* final game like all the other final games they'd played up until then, Julie agreed. They'd been going at it, nonstop, for almost three hours by then and, finally, she told herself, enough was enough.

At the same time, it occurred to Julie that she should lose the *final* final game—that she should let Buckley win the world championship.

Winning meant more to him than it did to her. It meant much more, in fact, than she'd imagined before she'd started going out with him.

Before she'd gotten to know him better, Julie had always imagined, from the way Buckley kept himself apart from everything that was going on at school—from sports and clubs and dating and everything—that winning and losing didn't mean all that much to him.

But as she'd gotten to know him better, she'd discovered that wasn't so. The truth was, winning meant so much to Buckley, unless he was pretty sure that he could win, he simply wouldn't bother to compete.

Like when he was in *The Philadelphia Story*.

He'd told Julie that he'd been so bad at rehearsals and so sure he'd make a fool of himself when it came time to perform that—right up until the last minute—he was seriously considering just walking out.

In fact, he told her, after he'd gotten through that disaster of a dress rehearsal, he was all ready to walk out the door and let Patriciana play the part.

In fact, he told her, if she hadn't called him down to the cafeteria for that last-minute "coaching session," he would have.

He'd come that close.

He was that competitive.

Julie *wasn't* that competitive. At least, that's what she told herself.

On the other hand, she told herself, Ping-Pong *was* her game. At least as much as any game was.

So, if Buckley was going to beat her at it, she decided, he'd have to beat her fair and square.

Telling herself that Gloria Steinem would be pleased with her decision, she tossed the ball in the air and banged her first serve over the net.

From that moment on, with both Julie and Buckley playing their hardest and best, the battle for the world championship was fast and furious.

All through the game, as they worked their way up to the final point, the lead kept seesawing back and forth between them.

Finally, with the score 20–19 and Buckley serving for the game, Julie returned one of Buckley's put-away slams —but she returned it so high that she set him up for another one.

As Buckley set himself to bang the ball home, Julie retreated from the table.

But, as she did—for probably the first time in the twenty games they'd played—Buckley resisted the urge to kill and, instead, he just teased the ball over the net.

Too far from the net to even bother trying to reach the ball, Julie watched as it dribbled across the table, bounced on the floor, and rolled away.

Obviously pleased with himself, Buckley smiled his championship smile.

"Best out of a hundred?" asked Julie.

Buckley laughed and shook his head.

"We should get back to the party," he said.

"Party?" asked Julie.

It was a fair question.

By the time they got upstairs to the living room, most of the crowd had gone.

Where they'd gone—whether they'd gone home or just upstairs—Julie couldn't tell.

There were still a few people hanging around the living room, but hardly anybody was dancing anymore. It was like all the drinking and smoking had tired everybody out. People were just sitting around, doing more of the same.

"Looks like the party's over," said Julie.

"Not until you've seen the nursery," said Buckley.

Julie looked at him.

"You've got to see it," said Buckley. "It'd be like going to Paris and not seeing the Eiffel Tower."

"Where is it?" asked Julie. "Upstairs?"

"In the attic," said Buckley.

"Way upstairs!" said Julie.

Buckley smiled.

"Beyond upstairs," he said. "It's really neat. Come on."

"I don't want to be a pill," said Julie. "But—"

"Good," said Buckley. "Come on."

He took her hand.

She went with him.

Up the winding staircase to the second floor.

Along the second floor hallway—past the closed doors with the muffled sounds behind them.

To a door at the end of the hallway.

Through the door and up a steep flight of stairs to the attic.

Through the attic—dusty and packed with racks of clothes and steamer trunks and crates and cartons—to another door.

"This is where Vicki used to hang out when she was a kid," said Buckley. "Before her father took off."

He opened the door on a room from another century—a playroom for a little girl from long ago.

There were framed illustrations from children's books and fairy tales hanging on the walls.

There were stuffed animals and dolls with porcelain faces lined up along the shelves.

There were toys—a child's tea service, a baby-size easel and paint set, a doll-size bassinet—in every corner.

There were lace curtains tied back with silk ribbons at the windows, lace-trimmed cushions on the seats of the antique chairs, a pink and white comforter on the little antique bed.

It all looked so perfect, so like a room in a museum, that Julie was reluctant to step inside.

"Are you sure it's all right?" she asked.

"Sure," said Buckley. "She still uses it."

"For what?"

Buckley laughed.

"Not what you think," he said.

"Uh-huh," said Julie. "And you and Vicki never . . . ?"

"Are you kidding?" asked Buckley—like the very idea was so totally ridiculous, it was crazy of Julie to even ask. "She *likes* me."

"So?"

"So she wouldn't want to complicate our friendship."

"How do you know?"

"She told me."

"Then you talked about it."

"Sure. I mean, not about doing it. With each other. But about it. Sure. We've talked about a lot of things. We're friends, kind of."

"Kind of."

"When we're together. Which isn't all that much."

"So you say."

"Are you jealous?"

She had to think about that. Especially after last night. When she saw Buckley dancing with Debra Stone, had she been jealous of Debra or was she just angry with Buckley?

She'd been angry with Buckley, she decided.

And later on, when the dance was over and Buckley explained to her how Debra had signaled him to rescue her from the clutches of Howie "The Hulk" Hogeboom—even though she still wouldn't trust Debra any farther than she could throw her—she hadn't been angry with Buckley anymore.

But what about Vicki?

What about this "friendship" between Buckley and her?

Was Julie jealous of that?

"Yes," she told Buckley.

Buckley smiled.

"Do *you* want to talk about it?" he asked. "About doing it?"

"No," she told him.

"Do you want to *do* it?"

"No."

He laughed. Kind of.

"Leave it open," she said.

Buckley had inched his way back over to the door.

"Please."

"Sure," said Buckley, looking both innocent and hurt at the same time.

Julie turned away from him and walked over to the lace-curtained window.

Looking out the window, out over the backyard, the pool and the pool house, she saw the star-studded sky, like a cape of darkest purple, draped over the ridge of black mountains that rose beyond the fields and forests at the edge of town.

She really liked Buckley. More than she'd ever liked anybody before. A lot more.

But do I love him? she wondered.

How can you know that, that you really love somebody, when you've never loved anybody before?

You can't, she told herself.

But you have to, she told herself.

You just know, she told herself.

How? she asked herself.

You just do, she answered herself.

Is this it? she asked herself.

She felt Buckley's hand at her waist.

She heard his voice, close to her ear.

"Pretty, isn't it?"

She leaned back against him, felt his cheek next to hers, breathed in the scent of his aftershave lotion.

"I like the night," she said.

"I like you."

"I like you, too."

"I more than like you."

She turned and kissed him.

"I more than like you, too."

He took her hand and led her to the little bed.

"The door," she said.

He closed the door and sat beside her on the little bed.

"I love you," he said.

And he kissed her.

And leaned her back.

And he was on top of her.

And his hands were all over her.

And she didn't care.

It felt so good.

"Please," he said. "There's nothing to be afraid of."

"I know."

Except getting pregnant, she thought.

"I brought protection."

There's nothing to be afraid of! she thought.

She'd never been particularly proud of being a virgin. She'd always thought of it like being a member of a club —like the Record of the Month Club.

It was no great honor. And being in it didn't say very much about what kind of person you were.

All it said about you is that you hadn't yet gotten around to doing something that you'd almost definitely get around to doing, sooner or later, anyway.

Like going to Europe, she'd thought.

But still, whatever she'd thought before, this was different.

This was the first time that what she thought really mattered.

"We can't just keep doing this," said Buckley.

"I know."

"I can't take it."

"I know," she said. "I can't, either."

"So what are we going to do?"

"I'm afraid."

"Don't be."

She knew it didn't hurt. No more than a bee sting or a tetanus shot, she'd heard. So it wasn't that she was afraid of.

What *was* she afraid of?

That he'd think less of her? Think she was fast or loose or something? That she'd lose him because she'd let him make love to her?

That didn't make sense.

What then?

That somebody might walk in on them? Up here?

Not likely.

"I want to be undressed," she said.

"Okay," he said.

He reached for the collar of her blouse.

She took his hand.

"No," she said. "I mean, I want both of us to be undressed. To get undressed."

"Oh."

"Buckley?"

She looked in his eyes.

"Are you sure?"

He looked in her eyes.

"Do I have to tell you?"

His eyes, the way he looked at her, said more than any words could.

"Kiss me?"

Still looking in her eyes, ever so slowly, he brought his mouth to hers and kissed her, with such sweet yearning, she felt her last doubt melt away.

"Up," she said.

Propping himself up on his elbow and trailing his fingers over her breasts, he rolled away from her and leaned back against the wall.

She looked up at him, for just a moment, memorized his smile, and then, turning away from him, she swung her feet to the floor and stood.

Keeping her back to Buckley, she walked over to the switch, on the wall next to the door, switched off the light, and then walked over to the window.

Standing in the moonlight, looking out at the starry night, she stepped out of her shoes and slowly began to undress.

Her blouse, her slacks, her panty hose, her panties—

one by one, she took them off and piled them neatly on a little antique chair.

Naked, she stood a moment by the window, feeling the tingle of the air on her skin, then—taking a deep breath to calm herself—she turned around.

"You're beautiful," said Buckley.

He smiled at her from the bed, where he waited, undressed, beneath the pink and white comforter.

"Thank you," she said.

It sounded silly, but she didn't know what else to say.

"Thank *you*," said Buckley.

He held back the comforter for her as she climbed into the bed and lay beside him.

As he pulled the comforter up around her, she said, "You're beautiful, too."

He smiled and said, "You must be in love."

She kissed him and said, "I am."

Twenty-four

It was like a dream, fluid and slow-motion, silent and perfect.

Neither of them said a word, not a word until the end, when she said, "Ohhh," and he whispered, "Sara Beth."

Then she was lying in his arms—her eyes closed, her long black hair spilling over his shoulder, her head against his chest, rising and falling with his breathing.

After that he must have dozed off, because, when he awakened, she was gone.

If he'd awakened in his own room, he might have thought he'd been dreaming.

But he awakened in a strange room, in a strange bed, and on the pillow next to him he saw a single, long, silky black hair.

So it was true.

And this is Sara Beth Cavanaugh's bed, in Sara Beth Cavanaugh's bedroom, in Sara Beth Cavanaugh's summer house, somewhere high on a mountaintop, an hour's drive north of New York City.

It's Saturday morning, the Saturday before Thanksgiving.

After a week of practicing for the Hoover game, the game for the league championship, which is to be played on Thanksgiving Day, the team has been given the day off.

The coach wants everybody in a good frame of mind for the big game.

And so does Sean.

Because a man named Bennett Edwards is going to be among the fans attending the game.

Mr. Edwards is a scout from Yale University and he's coming down from New Haven to watch Sean demonstrate his talents on the field of play.

Sean intends to give him an impressive demonstration.

By now, Sara Beth has pretty much convinced him that spending four years with "really first-class people" in a "really first-class school" wouldn't be a total waste of his time, no matter what he eventually decides to do with his life.

And since Yale is one of the classiest of the "really first-class schools" and its ivy-covered halls are jam-packed with "really first-class people," come Thursday afternoon, Sean intends to "Do or Die for Dear Old Yale!"

But that, he reminds himself, *is Thursday, Thanksgiving Day. And this is Saturday, Sara Beth Cavanaugh Day.*

Coming up here today was Sara Beth's idea.

When Sean told her about having the day off and how he had to get himself in a good frame of mind for the big game, Sara Beth said she knew the perfect place to spend the day and the perfect activity to put him in a good frame of mind.

Her parents had this summer place, she said, that they always closed up after Labor Day.

She could "borrow" her father's car from the garage where he parked it—he almost never drove anymore, she said, and she'd "borrowed" it before—and they could drive up for the day.

It sounded perfect to Sean.

And it would have been perfect.

If that had been all there was to it.

But there was more to it than that.

Sara Beth did the driving.

It was her car. Her father's, really. A big Mercedes.

169

Which she was used to driving and which she felt responsible for.

So she drove and Sean sat beside her and fiddled with the radio and checked out the view.

They'd gotten out of the city early, around eight-thirty. They wanted to make the most of their time together.

By nine o'clock, the city was behind them and the country was opening up before them.

Sean had WNEW-FM on the radio, and right on cue, they were playing Canned Heat's "Goin' to the Country" and everything was very good and rapidly getting better.

And then, from out of nowhere, Sara Beth said, "He's coming home."

Sean looked at her.

"For Thanksgiving," she said.

He wasn't surprised.

He knew Jack would have to come home, sometime— Thanksgiving, Christmas, Easter.

He'd kind of hoped he'd make other plans—skiing in Colorado, scuba diving in the Caribbean, wind sailing on the moon, whatever.

But he knew it was an idle hope.

If he was in Jack's shoes, nothing short of death or madness or total amnesia would keep him away from Sara Beth for one second more than he had to be.

So it wasn't surprising that Jack would return.

But nonetheless, the news that he was returning hit him like a kick in the gut.

He's coming home, he thought.

"You mean Jack?" he asked.

If they were going to talk about him, he decided, they might as well use his name.

Sara Beth nodded.

"Tuesday night," she said. "We're going out Wednesday night. Thursday, after the game, he's having Thanksgiving dinner with me and my family."

"Oh?" said Sean. "And what are you doing Friday?"

It came out a little sharper than he intended.

"I don't know."

"Saturday?"

"He's supposed to go back Sunday."

Sean knew he had no right to be angry, but he couldn't help it.

"Well," he said, "be sure and say hello for me."

Sara Beth looked like he'd slapped her face.

"Sean," she said. "Don't be that way. It's hard enough the way it is."

She was right and he knew it.

None of this was her fault. It wasn't anybody's fault, really. It just happened.

But here he was, taking it out on her.

He felt like a shit.

He reached over and put his hand on Sara Beth's shoulder and brushed the hair from her cheek and kissed the hollow between her neck and shoulder.

"You're right," he told her. "I'm sorry."

She reached over and put her hand on his knee.

"Anyway," she said, "we've still got today."

Sean put his hand on hers.

"Step on it," he told her.

It was a little after nine-thirty when they arrived.

By the time they got the house opened up and the water and heat turned on, it was ten-thirty.

Then they made love.

Twice.

And then he must have dozed off.

Now, he looks at his watch.

It's 12:16 on what looks like a crystal-clear, bright and sunny late autumn day.

Sean rolls out of bed and pulls on his jeans and wanders out to look for Sara Beth.

171

As he enters the living room, he sees her through the sliding glass doors that open out onto the sun deck.

She's leaning on the deck's split-wood railing, looking out over the sparkling lake at the foot of the mountain to the range of mountains that stretches off to the distant horizon, as far as the eye can see.

Just looking at her—lost in thought, eyes on the horizon, the wind playing in her hair—Sean feels a surge of tenderness so strong and deep, it brings tears to his eyes.

Sara Beth is all he's ever wanted.

Sara Beth is everything he needs.

As he slides open the glass door and steps out onto the deck, she turns to him.

She smiles to see him, without a shirt and barefoot, wearing nothing but his jeans.

"It's freezing!" she says.

"You have to tell him."

Her smile fades before his eyes.

"Tell him what?"

"That you love me."

She sighs and turns and looks away.

He walks over to her and stands behind her and rests his hand on her shoulder.

"Do you?" he asks. "Do you love me?"

She nods and says, "Yes."

"Will you?" he asks. "Will you tell him?"

She turns to him and looks into his eyes.

She nods and says, "Yes," and bursts into tears.

He takes her in his arms and holds her close.

"It will break his heart," she says.

"Yes," he tells her. "I know. I'm sorry."

"Oh, God!" she sobs.

He holds her closer.

He feels the tears burning in his eyes.

He can't hold them back.

He doesn't try.

Twenty-five

Happy Thanksgiving, she told herself.

The sound of the doorbell was still echoing around the house. It was Buckley.

Julie checked her watch. Seven o'clock. He was right on time, as usual.

She took one last look in the mirror, and then blushing at her own vanity, she tore herself away and hurried off to the door.

"Happy Thanksgiving."

They both said it at the same time—at the moment that Julie opened the door and saw Buckley standing there, grinning his Buckley grin.

They said it and immediately broke out laughing—partly because of how their minds worked the same way, but mostly because it wasn't really Thanksgiving. At least not as far as the rest of the world was concerned.

To the rest of the world, it was just plain old Saturday night.

But Julie and Buckley had their own ideas on the subject.

They wanted to spend Thanksgiving together. But Julie's parents were inviting her Uncle Larry and Aunt Linda and her twelve-year-old cousin, Catlyn, over from New York City for the day.

And Buckley and his parents always spent their Thanksgivings with Buckley's older brother and his family at their place in Marblehead, Massachusetts.

So there was no way.

Until they came up with the idea of celebrating their own personal Thanksgiving, a few days earlier than everybody else celebrated theirs.

They had a lot to be thankful for.

"Is that for me?"

"Oh," said Buckley. "Yeah."

He'd forgotten that he'd brought Julie a flower—a perfect red rose.

He'd forgotten because he was so blown away by how terrific Julie looked.

Julie saw how blown away Buckley was, and as she accepted the rose from him, she thought that just the look on his face made all the trouble she'd gone to worthwhile.

She'd bought a new dress because Buckley liked her legs and he said it was a shame that she kept them hidden under jeans and slacks all the time.

It was like a dress from the forties. It was silky and slinky. Black with bold swirls of white, it had big padded shoulders and a cinched waist and a slit that went up the side, almost to her hip, and a hem that fell just above her knees.

With her black stockings and her spiked heels and her hair flying out in all directions, Julie thought she looked like the fourth Pointer Sister.

But it was how she looked to Buckley that really mattered to her.

It was Buckley she'd dressed for, and she could tell that he liked the way she'd dressed for him by the way he was standing there, undressing her with his eyes.

As she lifted the perfect red rose and inhaled its musky sweet perfume and looked into Buckley's funny-sad eyes, Julie felt like Carmen in the opera of the same name.

"Beautiful," she said.

Looking into Julie's eyes, Buckley nodded and said, "Delicious."

He helped her on with her coat and waited while she locked up and walked her to the car and held the door for her as she climbed inside.

She watched him cross around in front of the car and thought about making love with him.

It seemed like, lately, that was all she ever thought about. God, it was beautiful!

It was beautiful the first time at Vicki's and even more beautiful the next time and the time after that—even though, both times, their bed was only a blanket, spread out in the back of Buckley's car.

It was fabulous!

In fact, making love with Buckley was *so* fabulous, Julie was actually beginning to worry about it.

She was beginning to worry that making love with Buckley was so fabulous, it might just crowd out all the rest of it.

It was so fabulous, she was afraid, instead of her and Buckley continuing to be friends and lovers, they might end up becoming just partners in sex.

If that happened, they would have lost everything that made their making love so fabulous in the first place.

Buckley climbed into the car next to her.

"Hungry?" he asked.

"Always," she answered.

"Thirsty?"

"I will be by the time we get there."

"Horny?"

"Drive!" she said.

He laughed. And then, as if he were a semipunk James Bond, he glanced over at her, lifted one suave eyebrow, and crooned, "My place?"

As if she were a blasé fourth Pointer Sister, Julie

glanced over at Buckley, sighed as if she couldn't care less, and said, "That was the plan, wasn't it?"

James Bond smiled and nodded.

"My place, then," he said.

He started up the car, squealed out of the driveway, and zoomed off in the direction of his house.

That *was* the plan—Thanksgiving for two at Buckley's house.

It was the plan that Buckley and Julie had come up with when Buckley's parents announced that they were spending the weekend in Atlanta, playing golf and looking into the possibility of opening up a branch of Discount Gourmet, which was the family business, and which—once Julie thought of it—was probably where Buckley had gotten his famous wok from.

But the really terrific thing about Buckley's parents taking off for the weekend was the fact that Julie's parents were taking off for the weekend, too.

Julie's mother and father were going into New York to see a show with Julie's Uncle Larry and Aunt Linda, and after the show they were planning to spend the night in the guest room at her uncle's rambling Fifth Avenue apartment.

Which meant, for their own personal Thanksgiving, Julie and Buckley had Buckley's house all to themselves and all night long to celebrate.

Buckley was taking care of everything. He was playing host and chef and chairman of the entertainment and cleanup committees.

All that Julie had to do was be ready when Buckley came to pick her up at seven—which she'd been.

And now, as they raced along the road, just to put everybody in a holiday frame of mind, Buckley punched up a cassette, and the next thing Julie knew, the car was filled with the sound of Mitch Miller and his Sing-Along Chorus singing:

> *"Over the river and through the woods*
> *To Grandmother's house, we go . . ."*

A moment later, following Mitch's instructions, Buckley was singing along.

A moment after that, although she considered her lush monotone a major embarrassment, Julie joined in.

They were still singing a few minutes later, when Buckley pulled into a driveway that curved around a rolling lawn and climbed to a landscaped parking circle at the back of Buckley's beautiful fieldstone, cedar, and glass house.

"Be it ever so humble," said Buckley, as he pulled the car to a stop.

Julie had never been to Buckley's house before.

"It's fantastic," she said, as she climbed out of the car.

The house harmonized so perfectly with its surroundings, it seemed to have grown right up out of the hilltop it commanded.

As Buckley showed Julie to the door, he joked about carrying her over the threshold.

"Is that a proposal?" Julie asked him.

Buckley smiled and shook his head.

"I'm too young to die," he said.

"Then I'll walk," said Julie.

Buckley opened the door for her.

Inside, the house was like the warmest, most comfortable ski lodge or mountain hideaway you could imagine. Although it was beautifully furnished and richly decorated, there was nothing at all standoffish about it.

"I love it," said Julie.

"Champagne?" asked Buckley.

Julie shrugged.

"If it was good enough for the Pilgrims," she said.

Buckley laughed and showed Julie into the den.

It was a great room—a glassed-in porch, extending out into a backyard that was landscaped like a Japanese garden, with little white stones and huge boulders, evergreen shrubs and trembling groves of white birch.

Buckley lifted the bottle of champagne from a silver ice bucket, wrapped a towel around it so it wouldn't drip, popped the cork, and poured the pale and effervescing wine into two delicate, narrow-stemmed glasses.

He handed Julie her glass and lifted his for a toast.

Looking into Julie's eyes, he said, "To the one and only Julie Stillwell."

He clinked his glass with hers.

"From the bottom of my heart," he said, "thank you."

Julie was so happy, she blushed.

"Any time," she said.

They drank.

Feeling the champagne buzzing, bittersweet and chilly, on her tongue, Julie closed her eyes and tried to memorize the sensation and the perfect moment of which it was a part.

"Help yourself to the hors d'oeuvres," said Buckley. "I need a second in the kitchen."

"Can't I help?"

"Uh-uh," said Buckley. "It's a surprise."

"It isn't turkey?"

"I didn't say that. Here. Something to soothe your weary mind."

He walked over to a stack of audio equipment and punched a button. Music poured out of the speakers on either side of the stack.

He smiled at Julie, and then he was gone.

Within ten minutes, he reappeared in the doorway.

"Grub," he announced.

There were more roses on the table.

And turkey—thin slices of turkey breast, baked and topped with prosciutto ham and melted cheese.

"Wow," said Julie, "is this good. Remind me to never cook for you."

They ate—the turkey, the buttery white asparagus, the plump potato gnocchi, the perfectly dressed green salad, and, for dessert, the fresh raspberries in heavy cream.

They drank—red wine for Buckley and grape juice for Julie, who'd poured herself a second glass of champagne while she was waiting and couldn't imagine feeling any better than she did.

They talked.

"Can I sing?" asked Buckley.

"You mean now?" asked Julie.

Buckley laughed.

"I mean in a play. On a stage."

"I don't know," said Julie.

"I can carry a tune," he said.

"Yes," said Julie. "But how far?"

"That's what I'm asking you."

"Why?"

Buckley shrugged.

"Because somebody wants me to be in a musical. To audition for a musical," he said. *The Fantasticks*. Ever heard of it?"

"Sure. I saw it. In New York," said Julie. "Who?"

"Arabella Alonzo."

Julie recognized the name. Arabella Alonzo was the head of the Short Hills Players, which was a community theater group that did a couple of shows a year in the theater at the Marymount School.

Julie couldn't remember them ever doing a musical before.

"They're doing *The Fantasticks?*" she asked.

"Yeah," said Buckley. "She called me. She saw me in

The Philadelphia Story and she thought, if I could sing, I might make a good El Gallo."

"She's right," said Julie. "If you're not too young for it. How old is she casting the girl?"

"I didn't ask her."

"I guess she must have somebody pretty young in mind."

Buckley shrugged.

"I bought the record," he said.

"Then you're going to do it?"

"I don't know," said Buckley. "I don't know if I can. Or if they'll want me to, after they hear me sing. I guess it'd be good to get the experience, though. I've only done one play."

"Not counting the Christmas Pageant," said Julie.

Buckley laughed.

"El Gallo's a juicy part," said Julie.

"I know," said Buckley. "I got the book out of the library."

"He's got some great songs."

Buckley cleared his throat.

"Want to hear one?" he asked.

"Sure."

"Okay," he said. "You wait here."

He pushed his chair back from the table, rose, and walked out of the dining room and back into the den.

Julie had a million thoughts.

She was really happy for Buckley.

She was happy that other people were starting to see him the way she saw him—not as the oddball he'd seemed like just a short while ago, but as an oddly appealing and really attractive young man, who might easily play the dashing hero of a young girl's dreams.

She was happy for herself, too.

She was proud of the role she'd played in discovering the real Buckley underneath the oddball and of the part she'd played in getting him the recognition that was starting to come his way.

But she wasn't really happy about his being in this new play. Not completely.

Because, to be completely honest about it, if Buckley was going to be in this new play, he'd have to spend a lot of time rehearsing for it, which meant he'd have a lot less time to spend with her.

She was really unhappy about that.

But she wasn't about to let Buckley know it.

Not now or ever.

She wasn't that selfish and she wasn't that stupid.

She would encourage Buckley to be all that he could be and hope that whatever else he would be, he would always be hers.

That's what she was thinking when she heard the music come pouring out of the den.

And then, there was Buckley. Or rather, there was El Gallo. Because when Buckley next appeared, entering through the door to the kitchen, he'd transformed himself into somebody Julie had never seen before.

Gazing out at her from under the floppy brim of a black Borsalino hat, Julie saw a handsome rogue, an experienced man of the world, who called himself El Gallo.

Reminded that Buckley could transform himself, so quickly and so completely, into someone else, someone she barely recognized, Julie felt a little thrill of excitement and fear.

And then he was singing—his voice rich and deep and filled with heartfelt emotion.

> *Try to remember the kind of September*
> *When life was slow and oh, so mellow . . .*

As he sang, Julie fell under El Gallo's spell.

Like the girl in the play—Luisa?—she felt so drawn to this handsome young stranger, she was ready to abandon the life she knew and follow him happily wherever he led her.

When the song was over, when El Gallo removed his hat with a sweeping gesture and bent his knee in a graceful bow, Julie was so deeply enchanted, it took her a long moment to remember where she was.

Then, as the hatless Buckley looked up at her from out of his deep bow, she said, "You'll be wonderful."

Buckley beamed.

"You think they'll take me?" he asked.

"They'd be crazy if they didn't."

"I don't know," said Buckley. "I don't know if I could do it. Without you. Directing me."

"You could," said Julie. "You don't need me."

Buckley grinned.

"Oh, yes I do!" he said.

"As a *director,*" said Julie. "When does it go on?"

"December thirteenth."

"In three weeks?"

"Three weeks from tonight."

"That's not much time."

"I know."

"That means you'd have a pretty heavy rehearsal schedule."

"Yeah. I know," said Buckley. "After school, every day. And all day on the weekends, she said."

"But we'd still have Friday and Saturday nights," said Julie. "Wouldn't we?"

"Yeah, I guess so," said Buckley. "But that's not much time."

It was practically no time at all, as far as Julie was concerned.

But she shrugged as if it didn't bother her and she looked Buckley up and down and she smiled and said, "I guess you're worth waiting for."

Buckley smiled.

"Have I told you how much I love you?" he asked.

"Not tonight," she told him.

Buckley's room was a long way from the den and his bed was a long way from the back of his car.

Julie and Buckley met between fresh-laundered sheets and made love as they never had before—once and then again, and after they'd slept a while, a third time.

Sometime, just before dawn, Julie awakened to the sound of music.

For a moment, she thought she must be dreaming, but no, she was awake and there *was* music playing and someone singing—Buckley!

The first light of day was seeping through the window as she climbed out of bed.

Borrowing a bath towel from Buckley's bathroom, she wrapped it around her and walked out onto the balcony overlooking Buckley's living room.

There in the living room below her, she saw him.

Standing before a wall of mirrors that threw his image back at him, wearing only his shorts and his black Borsalino hat, Buckley was singing:

> *Deep in December, it's nice to remember,*
> *Although you know the snow will follow.*
> *Deep in December, it's nice to remember:*
> *Without a hurt the heart is hollow . . .*

He didn't see Julie, standing on the balcony, above him.

> *Deep in December, it's nice to remember*
> *The fire of September that made us mellow . . .*

If he had looked, he might not have seen her.

> *Deep in December, our hearts should remember*
> *And follow . . .*

Before he'd finished, she was gone.

> *Follow, follow, follow.*

183

Twenty-six

When his alarm clock first goes off at six-thirty in the morning on Thanksgiving Day, Sean thinks it must be Sara Beth calling him.

But since his alarm clock sounds nothing like a telephone, he soon realizes it isn't the call he's been expecting since last night.

Sara Beth had promised she'd let him know how it went when she told Jack Ramsey that she was sorry, she couldn't help it, but she'd fallen in love with Sean Manning.

He'd waited up until one A.M. for her call, but it never came.

He'd told himself she'd probably gotten home sometime after midnight and decided it was too late to call. She'd call the first thing in the morning.

He'd told himself she'd decided that she still loved Jack. She was spending the night with him and wouldn't be home until morning.

He'd told himself that was nonsense.

Sara Beth loved him.

There was no way he could doubt it.

Not after last Saturday, at her summer house.

Not after the way she'd given herself to him so freely, so completely, so joyfully.

There was no way he could doubt it.

But still, she hadn't called.

And he'd hardly slept.

And ready or not, this afternoon at two P.M., he's going

to be playing the biggest game of his life—the Hoover game, the game for the league championship—and he's going to be playing it in front of Bennett Edwards, the scout from Yale.

I've got to get some sleep, he tells himself.

And he does.

He sleeps until he smells his mother's coffee brewing in the kitchen.

He awakens thinking, *She hasn't called!*

"Hello, Mrs. Cavanaugh. This is Sean Manning."

It's exactly nine o'clock. He's put it off as long as he could.

He's using the phone in his sister's room. The door is closed. He keeps his voice low.

"Excuse me for calling so early," he says, "but I need to talk to Sara Beth."

"She's not at home," says Mrs. Cavanaugh. "I'll tell her you called."

From the way she says it, he can tell she's about to hang up on him.

"Wait!" he says.

"Yes?" she says.

"When do you expect her back?"

"I don't know. She's going to a football game."

"That's not until this afternoon."

"I'm sorry," she says, although she hardly sounds it, "but that's all I know. They left about half an hour ago and I don't expect them back until dinner."

"Them . . . ?"

"Was there anything else?"

He wants to ask her who "they" are. Maybe she means Sara Beth and her father. Or maybe she means Sara Beth and somebody else that he's never even heard of.

But he knows who "they" are, and he's already tried her patience.

"No," he tells her. "Nothing else."

185

"I'll tell her you called."

"Thank you."

She didn't tell him! he thinks. *Why?*

The time wasn't right. Jack's first night home. She couldn't just—

Or maybe there were too many people around. A thing like that, you've got to find the right—

Anyway, he tells himself, *she's probably telling him right now. Taking a walk, probably. Maybe along the drive. Down by the river.*

Yeah. That's how she'd do it. Not the first minute she saw him. Not in front of a lot of people. She'd wait until the time and place were right.

Which is why she didn't call last night. She hadn't told him yet.

She's telling him now. As soon as she's told him, she'll call and say it's done.

He hopes she'll call before he has to leave for school. He's due in the locker room at noon, two hours before game time.

At exactly eleven forty-five, he tries her again.

And gets her mother again.

Without straining to be cordial, she tells him again that "they" have gone out and "they" won't be back until dinnertime.

He tells her that he's sorry to have bothered her—which he isn't—and hangs up.

For one desperate moment, he panics.

For a split second, it is clear to him that he is totally alone in the universe, that he is completely helpless, that his life has no meaning, that his death will touch no one.

For an instant, he wants to scream.

Or cackle.

Or wail.

"God!"

He says it out loud.

186

And then, slowly, reality begins falling back into place around him.

And he's okay.

Or he will be.

Yes.

He's okay.

"Jesus!"

He shakes his head to clear it.

He fixes his mind on the game.

It happens on the third play from scrimmage.

After two running plays go nowhere against the tough Hoover line, on instructions from the coach Sean calls for a screen pass.

The idea is, Sean will take the snap from center, drop straight back about ten yards, lob a short pass over the heads of Hoover's onrushing linemen and into the hands of his halfback, who will be playing possum, waiting for the ball just five yards in front of him.

It's a good idea on paper, but on turf it doesn't work.

Anticipating a pass, Hoover's coach calls for an all-out blitz and rushes all of his defensive backs against the Kenyon line.

At least two of them get through.

One man, coming from the left, hits Sean around the ankles while at the same moment another man, coming from the right, hits him around the thighs.

As he goes down, Sean feels his knee twist and wrench. He hears something pop and tear. He hears himself cry out. And then everything goes black.

Ammonia.

He smells it and jerks his head away.

He's awake. He wishes he wasn't. He's in agony.

Scarlet-colored lenses have dropped over his eyes.

There's a screeching inside his skull.

"Hang on, son."

His father takes his hand.

The screech of the siren, as the ambulance springs into motion, matches and amplifies the screeching inside his skull.

Every bump in the road, every jostle, is like a dagger in his knee, like a cleaver, like an ax.

Jesus!

"Easy."

In the emergency room at Roosevelt Hospital, they lift him onto the table.

"Dislocation," says the doctor to his father.

"Son?" he says. "Are you with us?"

Sean nods.

"We're going to give you something for the pain and then we're going to snap your knee back into place."

Sean shakes his head.

"Nothing for the pain," he says.

"It's going to hurt like a son of a bitch."

"Do it. Fast. Please."

The doctor nods and turns to Sean's father.

"Step outside please," he tells him.

"Are you sure this is the best—"

"Dad!"

"Yes," says the doctor. "Please."

"I'll be right outside, Sean."

The doctor takes off his jacket and rolls up his sleeves.

"Okay, son."

He puts his hands on Sean's leg and—

"How are we doing?"

Sean blinks his eyes.

The doctor is standing over him.

"Where is . . . ?"

"You passed out," the doctor tells him. "This is your room. For a day or two. Until the swelling goes down.

"You had a dislocated knee, a bad one. We popped it back into place, but there's some damage to the cartilage. Probably extensive damage."

188

"But nothing that can't be fixed," says his father. "I mean, he can come back from this, right? He can play ball?"

"It's possible," the doctor tells him. "But I couldn't say it's likely. We'll know more about what's possible and what isn't after surgery.

"My name's Lieberman, by the way, Arnie. Big game today?"

"Yes."

"That's tough," says Dr. Lieberman. "Well, you'll want to get some rest. I'll look in on you in the morning."

"Thanks."

"I'm sorry, son."

"Thank you, Doctor," says Sean's father.

"They do great things with knees these days," says Sean's father. The doctor is hardly out of the room and he's come over to the side of Sean's bed.

"It's okay."

"Sure it is," says his father. "It will be."

He takes Sean's hand.

"I tried to reach your mother, but Diana said she'd gone to a movie."

"She always said this was bound to happen someday," says Sean.

"I sent Diana home to wait for her," says his father.

"She said she couldn't stand to just sit there and watch," says Sean. "Anybody else?"

His father looks at him.

"Did anybody else show up yet besides Diana?"

"No," says his father. "But I guess the coach will, once the game is over. And maybe Mr. Edwards."

Sean shakes his head.

"The season's over," he says. "Maybe for good."

"Hey," says his father. "Don't talk like that."

"I need a telephone."

"I'll get you one," says his father. "And a TV. Only don't talk like that. Don't think like that. We'll beat this."

Suddenly, it occurs to Sean that a telephone might not be the best answer to his problem. The conversation he needs to have with Sara Beth may be too important to have on a telephone.

"Could you leave me some money, too?" says Sean. "For magazines. Snacks."

"Sure," says his father. "But I'm not going anywhere."

But Sean reminds his father that it's Thanksgiving and he's made plans to spend it with his current "favorite lady."

"There's nothing to do here but watch me sleep," he tells him.

After a while, his father lets himself be persuaded.

Before he goes, he puts twenty dollars in the bedstand, next to Sean's bed.

As he does, Sean sees that there are tears in his eyes.

Sean hasn't seen tears in his father's eyes since that morning, four years ago, when his father gave him his camera.

"It's okay, Dad."

"Sure it is," says his father. "When the going gets tough . . ."

"Get going," says Sean.

"Yeah," says his father.

And he leans over the bed and kisses Sean.

And then, without another word, he turns and heads out the door, waving over his shoulder as he goes and never glancing back.

Some time later a pretty nurse walks into the room.

She smiles and says, "Good morning."

Sean has dozed off.

"What time is it?"

"About six," says the pretty nurse. "Why? Are you planning on going somewhere?"

"No," says Sean.

"I wouldn't," she says. "It's a nasty night."

She's got a thimbleful of pills for Sean and a glass of water. Sean asks her if she can get him a telephone.

"It takes twenty-four hours to get it set up," she says. "From the time you ask. But if it's really important, I guess I could make a call for you."

"Thanks," says Sean. "But I don't think so."

"Lucky girl," says the pretty nurse.

And then she's gone.

And Sean spits out the pills that he was supposed to have swallowed but only stored in the corner of his mouth.

He looks over at his uniform, hanging in the little closet by the door.

He reaches over to his bedstand and slides open the drawer and takes out the twenty-dollar bill his father left him.

He reaches down and lifts the ice packs from around his knee, inches over the edge of the bed, slides his good foot out from under the sheets and plants it on the floor.

He reaches back onto the bed and, gritting his teeth against the pain, he slides his injured leg over to him.

Taking a deep breath and then another, he reaches under his leg, lifts it, swings it clear of the bed, and places his other foot on the floor.

The pain is so sharp, so exquisite, he nearly passes out.

But he grabs onto the bed and holds on to it until his vision has cleared and his stomach has settled and his breathing has returned to normal.

And then, letting go of the bed, he begins hopping across the room—slowly, one hop at a time—to the closet.

It's snowing as the taxi pulls up to the handsome brownstone on East End Avenue.

Sean pays the driver and eases himself out the door.

Supporting himself on one foot—his other foot is bare

and dangles above the ground—he swings the door closed and watches as the taxi pulls away.

He turns and looks up at the house and sees the softly falling snow making a halo around the light above the front door.

He counts the twelve steps that lead from the sidewalk to the door and hops his way over to them.

Turning his back to the stairs, he sits on the second step and backs his way up the stairs to the landing.

Grabbing onto the railing, he pulls himself up onto his good foot.

He rings the bell.

He hopes Sara Beth will come to the door.

Sara Beth's mother comes to the door.

She isn't happy to see him.

When she opens the door, Sean tells her, "I need to speak with Sara Beth."

"Sara Beth is eating her dinner," says her mother.

"I'll wait," says Sean.

"Suit yourself," says Sara Beth's mother.

She closes the door.

Sean doesn't know if he can wait. The pain in his leg is killing him.

He can't wait.

He rings the bell again.

He rings it, again and again.

Sara Beth opens the door.

She isn't happy to see him, either.

"What's that?" he asks her.

She's got an odd-looking piece of jewelry, like a tiny medal, pinned to her sweater, above her left breast.

"A fraternity pin," she tells him.

"Jack's?"

"Yes."

"What does it mean?"

She mutters something under her breath.

He doesn't understand.

"What?"

"Good-bye," she says.

"No!"

"I'm sorry," she says.

There are tears in her eyes.

"You're *sorry?*"

"I didn't mean . . ."

She shakes her head and looks away.

"The hell you didn't!"

"Sean?"

Jack Ramsey is walking down the hallway, coming to the door.

"Is that you?"

"You knew damned well what you were doing," Sean tells Sara Beth.

"I didn't!" she cries. "I don't!"

"Hey!" says Jack, arriving at the door. "What's going on?"

"Congratulations," Sean tells him.

Sobbing, Sara Beth turns and runs into the house.

Jack sets his jaw and glares at Sean.

"What have you done to her?"

Sean feels the tears starting to come, but he looks Jack in the eye and smiles and says, "Loved her."

Jack just looks at him, for a second.

Then he says, "Good night."

And closes the door.

Twenty-seven

She closed the book.

Finally.

Although she'd guessed it was Buckley calling when she heard the phone ring, she'd gone right on reading.

It was Thursday night and she had to get *The Great Gatsby* read and write a book report on it by next Monday.

Which might not seem like a lot—the book wasn't that long—but the writing was so good and the story was so heartbreaking she couldn't bring herself to hurry through it.

She couldn't get herself to put it down, either.

Until she heard her mother calling from downstairs.

"Guess who?" she called.

Then she closed the book and put it aside and lifted the phone and said, *"Buenos tardes, señor."*

"Buenas noches, señorita," said Buckley, correcting her.

Ten o'clock at night wasn't the time to be saying good evening.

"A thousand pardons, El Gallo," said Julie.

"De nada," said Buckley.

"You're too kind," she said.

Buckley laughed.

And then he said, "Listen . . ."

Julie knew what was coming. She couldn't say how. But she knew Buckley was calling to break their date for Saturday night and, what's more, she was already angry about it.

"Yes?" she said.

" 'Round and Round' isn't coming so good," he said.

Buckley's big second-act song had been a problem from the day rehearsals began, almost two weeks ago.

"It just lies there," he says. "And Arabella's no help. She thinks it's just dandy. That's what she says, after we ran through it tonight at rehearsal. 'Just dandy, boys and girls! Just dandy!' When everybody knew it was shit."

"Why?" asked Julie.

"Why is it shit?"

"Yeah."

"Kristin."

"What else is new?" said Julie.

Over the last couple of weeks, Buckley's leading lady had been the leading topic of conversation between them.

Kristin Erikson was a senior at Marymount, the Catholic girls' school where the Short Hills Players usually performed.

She was, according to Buckley, the All-American Girl, the Homecoming Queen, the Girl Most Likely to Succeed, and the People's Choice, all rolled up in one.

He couldn't stand her.

She was, he said, so pretty and smart and nice and popular that it was appalling.

He wouldn't have minded so much, he said, if she could act.

But she couldn't. Not at all. In fact, she didn't even try.

She was so pretty and smart and nice and popular that she didn't see any sense in getting up on a stage in front of people and pretending she was someone who was less pretty and smart and nice and popular than she was.

She could *sing*. Buckley admitted that. Like a bird.

Only, for some reason, when it came time for her to sing 'Round and Round' with him—when El Gallo shows her just how rotten and heartless the world could be—she got all whiny about it and her singing got all violiny and it sank the song.

It just lay there.

"Yeah?" said Julie. "So?"

Buckley heaved a sigh.

"So, we thought—"

"You and Kristin?"

"It's our song," Buckley reminded her.

"Uh-huh."

"We thought we should go back to scratch," he said. "On our own. And see if we can't figure out a way to get it off the ground."

"On your own?"

"Yeah."

"Without Arabella around to tell you it's 'just dandy'?"

"Right."

"Just the two of you? You and Kristin?"

"Yeah."

"Saturday night?"

Sounding amazed at Julie's having guessed what he was leading up to, Buckley said, "Yeah . . . !"

"Where?"

"At her house."

"Uh-huh."

"It's the only time we've got," Buckley explained. "Kristin has to do something with her family after rehearsal Sunday night. Some church thing."

Julie doubted that Buckley's problems with "Round and Round" were as major as he imagined.

More likely, he was just giving in to preshow jitters.

He'd been panicking about one thing or another right from the start.

If it wasn't the director's lack of imagination, it was the other actors' hamminess.

He said he'd walk out on the show if he could, even at

this late date, but it was already such a catastrophe, it was like a car wreck that he couldn't take his eyes off.

At first, Julie had tried to assure Buckley that things probably weren't as bad as they seemed to him. But that only made him insist that things were even worse.

So she'd given up on trying to cool him out.

Until this thing blew over, she'd decided, she was just going to go with the flow.

"So you want to break our date?"

"I don't *want* to," he told her.

"No problem."

"You mean it?"

"You can't let 'Round and Round' just lie there."

"I knew you'd understand."

Julie could hear the relief in his voice.

"Oh, yeah," she said, gritting her teeth. "You can count on me."

Her irony was lost on him.

"But what am I going to do with the Whiner?" he asked.

"Oil her?"

"What?"

"Joke," she told him.

"Yeah," he said. "Well, this isn't. I don't know if it's her or the song."

Don't say it, Julie told herself.

"It's her," she said.

It just jumped out at her.

"You think so?" asked Buckley.

Suddenly he sounded defensive.

"I've seen the play," Julie told him. "And I've read it. And, yes, I can see how the girl *could* get whiny, when El Gallo forces her to take a look at the ugly side of life.

"But she could just as easily be astonished and repelled and angry at the way reality falls short of her dreams. There's nothing in the play that says she has to whimper about it. She could rage."

As if Julie had just invented the wheel, Buckley said, "That's right! That would put some life in it! Why didn't I think of that? Why didn't Arabella?"

Why didn't Kristin? Julie thought.

"God," said Buckley, "if only you were directing—"

"You can't have everything," Julie told him.

"No," said Buckley. "I guess not. God, I miss you."

"How do you find the time?"

He laughed.

"It's easy."

"Yeah," she said. "I know what you mean."

"Do you miss me?"

"A little," she confessed.

"A little?"

She laughed—although she didn't feel like it.

"Okay," she said, "if you want to know the truth, I miss you a lot."

She felt a lump in her throat as she said it.

It wasn't like she hadn't been seeing Buckley. She'd been seeing him, every day at school.

They'd even made love again, just last Saturday night—although she didn't want to think about that.

But even so, ever since Buckley started rehearsals, she'd felt lost.

"I'm sorry about Saturday night," said Buckley.

"This Saturday?" Julie asked. "Or last Saturday?"

Buckley took a breath.

"Both," he said.

Last Saturday night, they'd had their first real fight.

They'd gone to a party at Elaine Lorraine's. Elaine had played Buckley's wisecracking sidekick in *The Philadelphia Story,* and this was kind of a cast reunion party—although there were a lot of other people invited, too.

Anyway, as parties go, Elaine's was a pretty tame affair. Especially when compared to the party at Vicki's, which was the last party that Julie and Buckley had gone to.

At Elaine's party, people actually talked.

Or at least they would have, if Buckley had given anybody a chance to get a word in edgewise.

As it was, fresh from rehearsing all afternoon, Buckley hadn't been able to leave his work or his role behind him.

Like El Gallo, from the minute he walked in, he commanded center stage.

To anyone who'd listen, he held forth on the problem of being a serious actor, drowning in the shortcomings of a company of amateurs and clowns.

Julie realized it was only Buckley's insecurity talking, but she hadn't yet learned how deep his insecurity ran. So, when she tried to get him to pipe down and chill out, he got angry with her.

What did she know? She hadn't been at rehearsals! She hadn't lived through the horror of acting with people who didn't know the first thing about acting, or taking directions from a woman who didn't know the first thing about directing!

She wouldn't have to walk out on the stage, in just two weeks, knowing—no matter how hard she tried or how well she did—she was bound to be embarrassed in front of a theater, filled to the rafters with friends and strangers!

Julie admitted she wasn't playing El Gallo in the Short Hills Players' production of *The Fantasticks*, so she couldn't really know exactly what Buckley was going through.

But, she said, over the course of the evening, Buckley had done a pretty good job of communicating his experience to everybody—herself, included—whether they were interested in hearing about it or not.

She also said she was ready to leave, whenever Buckley was.

It was still pretty early, not much past ten o'clock, and despite Julie's obvious unhappiness with his behavior, Buckley was still so full of himself he took Julie's request as an invitation to get down to the real business of the evening—making love.

Ten minutes later, they were in Buckley's car and heading for Buckley's house.

Buckley said his parents were out for the evening and probably wouldn't be back until long after midnight.

Julie said she didn't want to go to Buckley's house.

Buckley didn't understand.

"It's been a week!" he said.

"I know," said Julie. "It's been a week for me, too. But where does it say we have to make love every week, whether we feel like it or not?"

"Is something wrong?" asked Buckley.

"No," said Julie.

"You just don't feel like it?"

"That's right."

"What if *I* feel like it?"

Julie shrugged.

"Look," said Buckley, "I don't know if you've noticed, but I'm feeling kind of rocky just now, you know? Kind of trapped? With nowhere to go but down? You know?"

"I know."

"So, I kind of hoped you'd see that," he said. "I thought if anybody would understand what I'm going through, it would be you. I thought, 'Well, maybe everything else is falling apart, but at least I can count on Julie.'

"Anyway," he said, "that's what I thought."

In the end, Julie let Buckley persuade her.

But there hadn't been much love in their making love that night, and when it was over—although Buckley was, once again, his old, sweet self—Julie felt for the first time like she'd let herself be used.

That night, when she got home, before she went to sleep, she promised herself—although she loved Buckley and wanted to be there for him when he needed her—it would never happen like that again.

200

But now, she told him, "I forgive you."

"For last week?" he asked. "Or this week?"

"Both," she said—although she knew the more honest answer would have been, "Neither."

"What about Saturday?"

"Go ahead."

"Are you sure?" asked Buckley. "Because if you really don't want me to, I can tell Kristin—"

"Tell her nobody likes a pouter," said Julie. "And, yes, I'm sure. If I have to give you up so you can be in a play, you might as well be good in it."

"That's what I was thinking," said Buckley.

"After all," said Julie, "one of these days I'm going to have to sit through it. If *that* date is still on."

"Hey!" said Buckley. "Give me a break."

"Reading," said Julie.

"Huh?"

"If you were wondering what I was up to when you called."

Buckley laughed.

"God, I *am* being a pig about this, aren't I?"

Julie answered with a weary sigh.

"Do you still love me?" Buckley asked her.

"Yes," said Julie. "Do you still love me?"

"Madly," said Buckley. "If I promise to mend my ways, can I pick you up in the morning?"

"Sure."

"I promise," said Buckley.

"Mm," said Julie.

"Good night, beautiful."

"Good night, handsome."

They exchanged kisses and hung up their phones.

For a moment, Julie just sat there at her desk, fiddling with her antique gold necklace and staring off into space.

She had no reason to be suspicious, she told herself. Buckley loved her.

And as far as sex was concerned, there wasn't anything Kristin could do for Buckley that she wasn't already doing.

Unless Buckley was bored with her!

But there was no reason to think that. Not after last Saturday night.

Buckley was aching for her last Saturday night.

Last Saturday night, he couldn't live without her.

No, she told herself. There was nothing to worry about. Buckley loved her.

If there was anything she was sure of, she told herself, it was that.

Twenty-eight

Blind. Blinded by the light. Springsteen must have been thinking about me, walking out of a dark theater in the middle of a bright December afternoon, when he wrote that.

Hobbling. Hobbling out of a dark theater on a bright— Wednesday? Thursday. Mid-week afternoon.

Sean shifts his crutches into neutral and wipes the tears from his eyes.

It's the bright sunlight, he tells himself, *the bright sunlight, bouncing off the dark gray snow.*

If anybody asks me why I'm crying, that's what I'll tell them.

"It's the sunlight, sir."

He says it out loud and looks around to see if anyone's noticed.

No one's noticed.

There are still a couple of people straggling out of the theater, but they're case-hardened New Yorkers, so they take no special notice of young Tim Cratchit, even though he's standing right on their doorstep, crying his eyes out and talking to himself.

Anyway, it isn't the sunlight that started him crying. It was the damned movie.

He can't believe it!

He can't believe he went to see *Shane* again, when he'd seen it two or three times before and knew perfectly well that it was about this beautiful, happily married frontier woman who falls in love with this handsome stranger who rides into town and saves her and her family from a pack of bloodthirsty villains.

How could he have forgotten that the movie ended with the beautiful woman choosing her husband and the life they'd made together over the stranger and the life they might have made?

Remind you of anything, jerk?

It was exactly what he didn't need.

He'd gone to the movies to forget about Sara Beth and not to be reminded that she'd chosen Jack over him.

It wasn't like he needed reminding. Going to the movies seemed to be about the only way he could forget about Sara Beth.

And avoid her.

He hadn't been back to school yet. Not since he'd gotten his knee wrecked. But as far as he could tell, he hadn't been missed.

His mother had called the school to tell them he was going to have an operation, so he guessed they probably thought he was still recovering from it.

But the truth was, he could have gone back to school last week, right after the surgery. The pain wasn't too bad and he could get around well enough on his crutches.

In fact, he'd started every school day since the surgery by packing up his books and saying so long to his mother —and his sister, if she was still around—and lumbering out the door, as if he were going to school.

And every night he lumbered back home and reported to his mother on how his day at school had gone.

But he never actually went to school.

He was afraid he'd bump into Sara Beth.

He *knew* he'd bump into Sara Beth.

And he was afraid, when he did, he might scream at her and grab her and shake her and shove her against a wall and—

Why did she do it?

Why did she pretend that she was in love with him?

Was he just something to do while Jack was off at school? A fun way of passing the time? A way of not being lonely?

Was she just out to prove to herself once and for all, before she settled on Jack, that she could have any man she wanted? Was he just another trophy on her shelf, another notch in her gun?

It didn't matter. He'd never mattered to her. She'd used him.

So when he bumped into her, he might scream at her and—

Or else he might fall on his knees and beg her to take him back.

He might do that, too. He loved her that much.

And maybe she wasn't pretending. Maybe she did actually love him.

But maybe she thought Jack had more to offer her. More than love.

Maybe she just needed Sean to tell her that he could offer her more than love, too. More than Jack could offer her.

So when he bumped into her, he might fall on his knees and—

But it would be one way or the other.

He couldn't imagine it going any other way.

Until he could, he wasn't going back to school.

He was going to the movies.

He'd been catching two a day most days for the last week and a half.

When he wasn't watching movies, he was at the hospital's rehabilitation center, working on his knee.

He checks his watch. It's almost four. He could shoot over to the rehabilitation center now.

But at the moment, he doesn't really feel like reexperiencing the pain he felt when the knee first got whacked out of joint—which is what it feels like every time he goes to the center and bends or flexes or lifts with his knee.

Although he's anxious to be rid of his crutches, he reminds himself that football season is over and tells himself that it won't matter if he misses a day of therapy.

So, his mind made up, he shifts his crutches into first and sets out for the nearest subway station.

He wonders how his father is doing in his search for a doctor with an optimistic outlook.

Dr. Cronin, the orthopedic surgeon who performed his operation, hadn't been optimistic.

With a lot of hard work and dedication, he said, Sean would be able to get his knee back into good enough shape for walking around on and leading what he called an "active life."

But he was afraid, no matter how hard Sean worked on strengthening his knee, it would never be as stable as it was before the injury.

Which meant that Sean would be susceptible to another dislocation.

If Sean suffered another dislocation like the first one, he said, there was a risk he might be lame for the rest of his life.

Sean was stunned.

He'd thought about giving up football anyway. So, he supposed, the doctor's diagnosis shouldn't have bothered him that much.

But being told that he might not have a choice, that he might not be fit to play, even if he wanted to, was something else.

He didn't know what to think.

His father knew what to think.

He thought Cronin was an "alarmist" and he told him so and then he set out on his search for a doctor with a more optimistic outlook.

He's still searching.

And meanwhile, when Sean isn't catching movies, he's working out.

And he's doing all right.

For example, taking the stairs down to the subway.

With two crutches under his left arm and his right hand on the railing, Sean practically flies down the stairs.

And he's fine on the train, too. People make a lot of room for a guy on crutches. Maybe because they think a guy on crutches is going to ask them for money or their seat or something.

And the ride up the escalator that takes him from the subway to the main floor of the Port Authority Bus Terminal is a breeze.

Sean hasn't come to the bus terminal to take a bus. He isn't going anywhere. Although he's thought about it.

It would be so easy. He's got about four hundred dollars in his savings account. He could take it out and come down here and buy a ticket to anywhere in the country—Los Angeles, New Orleans, San Francisco.

He's only seventeen. He's got his whole life ahead of him. He could chuck everything and everybody and start all over again somewhere else.

All he'd have to do is hop on a bus, and by the day after tomorrow he could be anywhere at all.

And who would miss him?

Not the Kenyon Crusaders.

Sean laughs at himself for thinking of them first.

But with Paul Lazar filling in for him as quarterback, they'd beaten Hoover 13–7 and won the league championship. So they hadn't missed him.

And his mother *wouldn't* miss him.

Things hadn't been the same between his mother and him since his mother asked his father to move out.

Even though four years had passed since then, his mother was still pissed at his father and, maybe because she'd always thought of Sean as his father's son, a distance had opened between them.

Except for the way it might look to people, Sean didn't think that his mother would mind if he made the distance between them geographical as well as emotional.

His sister wouldn't miss him, either.

With him gone, Diana would have her telephone and her mother all to herself.

His father?

His father would miss him. In fact, he was missing him already. He just didn't know it yet.

He was still counting on Sean's coming back from his injury. He was still looking forward to his playing big-time college football. He was still dreaming about all the scholarships and the trophies and the national championships that he'd set his heart on back when Sean was still a kid.

So, yes, if Sean took off and left his dreams to wither on the vine, his father would miss him.

Sara Beth?

Would she miss him?

Did she miss him now?

Why did she do it?

The question echoes in his mind as he moves through the crowded bus terminal and makes his way to his rented locker.

Fishing the key out of his pocket, he opens his locker and hauls out all his schoolbooks. He selects a few and puts the others back. Then, depositing four quarters in the slot, he retrieves the key from the lock, turns, and heads back down to the subway.

"Who's April?"

That's how his sister greets him when he walks through the door.

"Sean?"

That's his mother, calling from the kitchen.

"Hi, Mom," he calls back to her.

208

"Who is she?" asks Diana.

"April Addams?" Sean asks her.

She's the only April he knows. But why would she be calling?

"Your father called," says his mother.

She's standing in the doorway to the kitchen, sipping coffee and nibbling on a cookie.

"She said you could call back until one," says his sister. "One in the morning?"

Sean laughs and nods.

"April Addams," he says.

"He wants to see you before he goes off on his vacation," his mother says. "How was your day?"

"Fine," says Sean.

"Who is she?" asks his sister.

"Diana!"

"An old friend," he says.

"I'll bet," says his sister.

"Can I use your phone?"

Diana looks at her mother.

"It isn't mine," she says. "It's just in my room."

"Thanks," says Sean.

He doesn't know April's phone number. The information operator does. He dials her.

April picks up the phone on the first ring. She sounds like she's surprised that Sean's called her back.

He asks her what's up.

She tells him nothing. Or, actually, quite a lot. But that isn't why she called.

"How's the knee?" she asks.

"Coming along," he tells her.

"So I guess they must all be breathing a sigh of relief out at Notre Dame, huh?"

Sean laughs.

How does she know about Notre Dame? he wonders. *Archie Webber must have told her.*

"I don't think so," he says. "I can't play football any-more."

"No!"

That's not right, Sean tells himself.

"Well, actually," he says, "I'm not sure I can't play."

Cronin could be wrong.

"But," he says, "if the doctor who did the operation knows what he's talking about . . ."

But not that wrong.

". . . I won't play."

"God!" says April.

I'd be crazy to.

"That's pretty terrible, isn't it?" asks April.

Lame.

"No," says Sean. "I mean, I'll be all right. My knee will. But, yes, I guess it is. Terrible, I mean."

"What are you going to do?"

"When?"

"Come fall," she says. "Where will you go?"

"Oh," says Sean. "I don't know. I don't know where I'll be going in the fall. Or what I'll be doing. Or who I am. Or what I want to be when I grow up."

April takes a moment—letting it all sink in, Sean guesses—and then she says, "Well . . . I'm sorry about your not playing football anymore."

"Thanks," says Sean.

"You looked so cute in your uniform."

Sean laughs.

"But," she says, "if you're really as screwed up and lost as you say you are . . ."

"I am," Sean assures her.

"Well, it's about time!" says April, sounding like she's genuinely delighted to hear it.

"Everybody else I know has been screwed up forever," she says. "Welcome to the club!"

Sean laughs.

"Thanks," he says.

"You're much better off having your nervous breakdown when you're young," she says, "and getting it behind you."

Sean laughs again.

"Who said anything about a nervous breakdown?" he asks her.

"My shrink," she says. "I've started seeing one. In fact he's the only guy I am seeing right now. His orders.

"I can *see* other guys," she says, "but I can't go to bed with them.

"So they're not seeing me," she says. "Like your friend Archie Webber. It turns out he didn't love me for my personality. It turns out nobody did.

"I guess I have a lousy personality," she says. "But a great body, right?"

"I never had any complaints with either," Sean tells her. "So how long have you been seeing a shrink?"

"Since a couple of weeks ago," she tells him. "My parents came home one night when they weren't supposed to and caught me in bed with this married friend of theirs."

"Ouch!" says Sean.

"He was so unhappy," says April.

"Mm," says Sean.

"I've got low self-esteem, Sean."

"I'm sorry."

"And the fact that nobody's calling me since I stopped acting like the town pump isn't raising it any."

"Yeah," says Sean.

"Like, ask me what I'm doing New Year's Eve," she says.

"What are you doing New Year's Eve, April?"

"I thought you'd never ask!" she gushes. "I'd *love* to."

"What?"

"Anything," she says. "But."

Sean laughs and tells April, "It's a date."

211

"You mean it?" she asks.

"You can't kick a girl when her esteem is down," says Sean. "Not with a dislocated knee, anyway."

"You don't have any other plans?" she asks.

"New Year's is weeks from now," he says. "I don't know what I'm doing five minutes from now. I don't even know what I'm doing now."

"You're being very nice," she tells him. "Thanks."

And she hangs up on him.

Sean sits a minute, holding the receiver in his hand.

He tells himself, *Now I won't be able to take off on a Greyhound until after the first of the year.*

Then, catching himself getting sucked into his own dumb fantasy, he laughs and hangs up the phone.

Twenty-nine

He loves her!

She wanted to howl it.

He loves her!

She hurried across the Maymount campus, heading for the Walter Kerr Theater and the opening night of *The Fantasticks*.

There wasn't much doubt in her mind.

Buckley had fallen in love with Kristin Erikson, just the way he'd fallen in love with Kelley Seaver.

Okay, she told herself, *so maybe it isn't love.*

At least it wasn't the kind of love that she felt for Buckley. Real love. Maybe it was just infatuation.

He's infatuated with her!

No, it was more than that.

It wasn't just that he'd been ignoring her all this time. She knew he was busy with rehearsals and panicked about the way they were going.

She didn't mind that she hadn't seen him last night or today. She understood how he didn't want to be distracted when he was getting ready for a performance.

He wanted to concentrate all his energy on getting up for it. Like a fighter getting ready for a fight. She understood that.

She didn't mind his breaking their date, last Saturday, so he could rehearse with Kristin, either.

At least, not as much as she minded his not calling her,

like he always did, Sunday, during his lunch break, and telling her how it had gone.

At first, when he didn't call, she'd told herself he was probably rehearsing straight through lunch.

But she didn't buy it.

She knew Buckley hadn't called because he was feeling guilty about what had happened between him and Kristin the night before.

He was afraid, if he called, she'd hear the guilt in his voice.

But that wasn't what she heard in his voice when he finally *did* call, late Sunday night.

He said he'd rehearsed straight through lunch. Otherwise, he said, he would have called her.

He said he and Kristin had rehearsed "Round and Round" from eight o'clock until almost midnight, when Kristin's mother, who'd been home the whole time, said they were driving her crazy.

He said he'd given Kristin her suggestion—that she should try getting angry about how cruel the world was, instead of just whining about it, like she'd been doing.

He said Kristin had tried it and it made all the difference. Done Julie's way, "Round and Round" was a knockout and Kristin was fantastic.

He thanked Julie.

For himself and for Kristin.

He said, "I love you, Julie."

She said, "I love you, too."

And he said good night.

He didn't sound guilty.

But he *did* sound something just short of it.

There was something in his voice that made Julie think he might be telling her the truth, as far as he went, but he wasn't quite looking her straight in the eye.

It was nothing she could put her finger on.

But once she'd heard it, she started listening for it whenever they talked and it was always there.

He's in love with her!

She wanted to howl it.

Cut it out! she told herself, as she entered the lobby of the Walter Kerr Theater and joined the crowd filing into the auditorium.

You're just making it up, she told herself as she took her seat in the auditorium and exchanged smiles with the woman sitting next to her.

Buckley's in love with you and nobody else.

Didn't he tell you, just last night?

It was the last time they'd spoken.

Buckley told her he was scared.

Julie said she could understand how he would be.

But she also reminded him how much he loved pushing through his fear and walking out on a stage and performing in front of an audience.

"Yeah," he said. "I do kind of like that, don't I?"

"You love it," she told him.

"And you," he said.

"You sure?" she asked him.

"Cross my heart and hope to die," he said.

And she wanted to believe him.

More than anything.

If only she could.

As the houselights dimmed, she closed her eyes, and made a wish.

Let him be wonderful, she wished.

And not in love with Kristin.

She opened her eyes to the sound of music—a piano and a harp, playing the actors onto the stage.

He cut his hair!

That was the first thing she thought when she saw Buckley strut out onto the stage, dressed all in black and playing the dashing El Gallo.

Although all that he'd actually done was trim away the curls that slashed down over his forehead and even out the rest of his hair so that it looked short and neat all the way around, Julie barely recognized him.

The instant he hit the stage, he was the Dark Stranger that every girl dreams of, the Romantic Adventurer who will one day come for her and carry her away.

He was El Gallo!

And Kristin was Luisa.

God, is she ever! thought Julie.

If Luisa was supposed to be the picture of girlish innocence, captured at the moment before it exploded into ripe and womanly sensuality—which she was—then Kristin was Luisa to the teeth.

With her pale blond hair cascading down over her creamy white shoulders, her ice-blue eyes, her prominent cheekbones, her full and luscious mouth, her perfect breasts, narrow waist, and impossibly long legs, Kristin was breathtakingly beautiful.

The moment she saw her, Julie knew she was sunk.

And when Kristin joined Buckley in singing the opening song, when she added her angel-sweet voice to Buckley's smoky baritone, Julie thought she'd hit bottom.

And when the song ended and the play began and Kristin began flirting with her innocent young beau, Julie *knew* she'd hit bottom and fallen right through.

There was no room for doubt. Kristin was the girl every girl dreamed of being and every boy dreamed of having. She was simply irresistible.

Julie hated her!

But she couldn't take her eyes off her.

She couldn't even make herself pay attention to Buckley.

She didn't even see the other actors on stage.

She couldn't even follow the progress of the play.

She watched the whole first act, hypnotized, as if she were in a dream, and only when the act was over—when the houselights came up and the audience broke into applause—did she finally awaken.

Like a bat emerging from a pitch-black cave and flying into bright sunlight, Julie got up from her seat and began groping her way up the aisle to the lobby.

Even though she was awake, she was still in a daze.

She couldn't think of anything except how impossibly beautiful Kristin was.

Compared to her, Kelley Seaver was plain-looking!

Compared to her, Julie was—

Screwed!

When she reached the lobby, she bummed a cigarette from a guy and tried to smoke it.

But it made her cough until she cried and everybody looked at her.

As soon as she got her breath back and cleared her eyes, she snuffed the cigarette out and hurried back to her seat and waited for the second act to begin.

It was in the second act that the roguish El Gallo stole Luisa away from her innocent beau and took her off to see the world.

El Gallo and Luisa sang "Round and Round."

But most importantly for Julie, it was in the second act that El Gallo fell a little bit in love with Luisa and kissed her—on the eyes.

That was the moment Julie was waiting for and dreading.

She knew, right after they finished singing "Round and Round," Kristin would close her eyes and lift her face to Buckley and Buckley would lean down and kiss her on the eyes.

In that moment, Julie believed she'd be able to see

through Buckley's acting to his real emotions and know, beyond a doubt, if Buckley was really in love with Kristin.

So, as Act Two began, Julie crossed her fingers and waited for the moment of truth to arrive.

She didn't have long to wait.

Before she knew it, Buckley and Kristin were cavorting about the stage, singing "Round and Round."

And then the audience was applauding.

And then El Gallo turned to Luisa and said, "'Now hurry. You must pack so that we may run away.'"

And Luisa answered, "'Kiss me first.'"

"'All right,'" said El Gallo.

Julie held her breath.

Buckley reached out to Kristin and placed his fingertips ever so lightly on Kristin's cheeks.

Kristin closed her eyes and lifted her face to him.

Buckley leaned down to Kristin and, ever so tenderly, kissed her eyes—first one eye, and then the other.

But he didn't stop there!

He kissed her *mouth!* Even though *he wasn't supposed to!*

That wasn't how it was written in the play!

El Gallo wasn't supposed to *kiss* Luisa! Not her *mouth!* Just her *eyes!*

"'At last!'" said Kristin. "'I have been kissed upon the eyes.'"

God!

"'No matter what happens,'" said Kristin, "'I'll never never ever forget that kiss. I'll go now.'"

After me! thought Julie.

She felt her tears stinging her eyes and streaming down her cheeks—tasted her tears at the corners of her mouth.

"Excuse me," she whispered to the woman seated next to her.

"Excuse me." She mouthed the words to the man seated on the aisle.

As she hurried up the aisle and pushed through the door at the back of the auditorium, Julie felt a sob clawing at her throat, struggling to get out.

She gasped once, fighting to hold it back, as she hurried across the lobby and down the stairs to the girls' room.

As she bolted through the door of the girls' room, she couldn't hold it back any longer.

"Ohh," she sobbed. "Buckley! You *bastard!*"

Distorted and amplified, the sound of her sobbing echoed back at her from the room's white tiled walls.

How could you? she thought.

She walked over to the sink, looked at herself in the mirror.

How could you?

She bowed her head over the sink and sobbed.

It hurt her so!

He'd hurt her so!

"Bastard!"

She said it again.

And sobbed.

Pull yourself together!

She took a huge gulp of air and turned on the cold water and looked in the mirror.

Her eyes were a sight.

If he saw her this way—

What?

What difference would it make, now?

Plenty!

She cupped her hands under the faucet, collected a handful of ice-cold water, and splashed it on her face.

She wouldn't let him see her this way.

She wouldn't give him the satisfaction.

From far away, above her in the auditorium, she heard Buckley singing the show's final song:

Deep in December, it's nice to remember,
Although you know the snow will follow.
Deep in December, it's nice to remember:
Without a hurt the heart is hollow.

Deep in December, it's nice to remember
The fire of September that made us mellow.
Deep in December, our hearts should remember
And follow.

Follow, follow, follow.

As the auditorium above her erupted in applause, Julie dried her face.

She'd promised Buckley she'd come backstage after the show and go with him, after he'd cleaned up and changed, to the cast party at the Pinebrook Country Club.

She took a deep breath and set off to keep the first part of her bargain.

She wasn't the first to arrive backstage.

There was already quite a crowd. At the center of it stood Buckley and Kristin.

They were smiling and holding hands as they accepted congratulations from a line of well-wishers filing by.

The happy couple! thought Julie.

To her, Buckley and Kristin looked exactly like a bride and groom standing in a receiving line at the end of a wedding.

She didn't join the line.

Instead, she stood off to one side, watching Buckley and Kristin sharing their triumph, exchanging smiles and jokes and laughter with their well-wishers and each other.

Buckley was so busy accepting his fans' congratulations, he didn't notice Julie watching him.

She waited until the crowd around him began to thin out.

Then she steeled her nerves and made her move.

"Julie!"

Buckley took her hand and drew her to him and kissed her, coolly, on the cheek.

Then, turning to Kristin, he said, "Kristin, this is—"

"I heard!" said Kristin.

She was even more beautiful offstage than on—even more beautiful close up than far away.

"Our favorite director!" she said, taking Julie's hand.

Our? thought Julie.

"Thank you for saving my life," said Kristin, embracing Julie.

"And Roy's," she added.

Roy's?

"If it wasn't for you," said Kristin, "I would have brought him down to my level."

Buckley grinned and blushed.

"Well, almost," Kristin said, laughing.

She squeezed Buckley's hand and drew him closer to her.

"So, what did you think?" she asked Julie. "You can't imagine how much your opinion means to me. After all Roy has told me about you."

"I think you're terrific," said Julie. "I think you *were* terrific. In the show, I mean. Both of you. Terrific!"

"Me, too."

A young priest was standing at Julie's side.

"Excuse me," he told Julie, "but I just had to tell these two people how much I enjoyed their performances."

"Sure," she told him. "I was just leaving anyway."

"Meet you in the lobby?" she asked Buckley.

"Yeah," he said. "Sure. You really liked it?"

221

"Loved it," she said.

Bastard!

Buckley beamed as she turned and walked away.

It took about half an hour for him to clean up and change.

Julie passed the time alone in the lobby, examining the posters for the Short Hills Players' previous productions and wondering what she'd do with herself, now that her life was over.

She didn't cry. She was past tears. She was past all emotions.

She was like a wounded jet pilot, flying a damaged plane through a storm. Knowing she might crash any second, she was somehow, by God's mercy, miles above it all.

After what seemed like an eternity, Buckley appeared. All dressed up and ready for the cast party, he was smiling his classic Buckley smile and acting like—except for his haircut—he was the same old Buckley.

"Hi, pretty," he said, as he crossed the lobby to Julie.

"Hi, Roy."

He laughed.

"She does that to bug me," he explained.

"Sweet," said Julie.

Buckley put his arms around her and kissed her.

Julie told herself she felt nothing.

When the kiss was over, she turned her face from him and blinked away her tears.

Buckley didn't notice. He took her hand and led her to his car. He did all the talking.

The show had come off a lot better than he'd ever expected.

For one thing, he'd never expected Kristin to be as incredibly good as she was.

She was at least ten times better than she'd ever been in rehearsals.

Fabulous.

222

Which, of course, did a lot for Buckley's performance.

He'd been better than he'd ever been, too.

And so, he guessed, had everybody else.

"Did you hear that audience?" he asked.

"Are you in love with her?"

They were in the car by now—on the road, heading for the Pinebrook Country Club and the cast party.

Buckley kept his eyes on the road.

"Who?"

Julie said nothing.

"Kristin, you mean?"

He glanced over at Julie.

"I don't know," he said.

"You don't *know?*"

She felt her tears again, burning, hot and angry, in her eyes.

"I don't," he said. "I know I love you. I know that. You know that, too, don't you? I do, Julie. I love you. I swear."

She turned her eyes from him. She looked out her window at the houses passing by.

"How long?" she asked.

"How long, what?"

"How long have you known? Did you know the night of Elaine's party?"

"I don't know *now!*" he insisted.

She said nothing.

"I'm sorry," he said.

"Have you—?"

She stopped herself.

She didn't want to know.

"No," he said. "Of course not!"

"Of course not?" she asked him.

"She's not that kind of girl."

She just looked at him.

When he turned to her—when his eyes met hers—she said, "Take me home."

Thirty

"I like traveling, all right," says Sean's father. "I just don't like being away from home."

"Well," says Sean, "it's only two weeks, right?"

"Ten days," says his father. "I'd have settled for a week, myself. But Chrissie says you can't get a week off in less than ten days and she needs a week off."

"So you're taking ten days," says Sean.

"Have some guacamole," says his father. "I bought it myself."

"Thanks," says Sean.

They're sitting in the conversation area at his father's bachelor pad, just the two of them, hanging out before dinner, talking vacations and guacamole.

Sean's father is going on one and serving the other.

Sean hasn't got much to say about either, but he'd rather talk about them than lots of other things.

Like his father's exercise bicycle, for example—the handsome, European-designed black matte-finish exercise bicycle that stands in the corner of the living room, looking like a piece of ultramodern sculpture.

Sean's father has owned it for a while and Sean has admired it. But right now, Sean's pretending it isn't there.

He doesn't want to get into a conversation about exercising. He's afraid of where it might lead.

So far, he hasn't said anything to his father about not playing football anymore, although—by now—there's no doubt in his mind that his football-playing days are behind him.

He's been trying to think of a way to break it to his father that won't just wipe him out.

And so far he hasn't been able to come up with one.

So whenever his father's gone on about how great things are going to be when Sean gets back to his old self and starts tossing the old pigskin around again, Sean hasn't stopped him.

He's warned him not to get his hopes too high. But he hasn't stopped him.

"Hungry?" asks his father.

"Yeah," says Sean.

"Good," says his father. "Because I got you a steak as thick as that."

"Dinner of champions!" he says.

Sean laughs.

"Great," he says.

"You like it, don't you?"

"Steak?" asks Sean.

"My bike."

"Oh," says Sean.

His father's caught him staring at the damned thing.

"Yeah," he says. "It's great."

"It's yours."

"No," says Sean. "Thanks."

"I want you to have it," says his father. "For your knee. You can work out on it. Right at home. Anytime you want."

"Right," says Sean. "Twenty-four hours a day, if I want."

"Well," his father says with a smile. "You've got to sleep."

"And eat," says Sean.

"You don't have to stop for that," says his father. "You can eat and pedal at the same time."

"Great," says Sean.

"You've got a lot of work to do, if you want to play ball in the fall, right?"

"Definitely," says Sean.

"And anyway," says his father, "I've got inside information that Santa Claus is bringing me a bike that I saw in the Sharper Image catalogue. It's got a built-in computer. Tells you all kinds of things—pulse rate, exchange rate, miles per gallon."

"Dad," says Sean.

"Nope," says his father. "I don't want to hear any more about it. It's yours."

"Don't you think it's about time you stopped believing in Santa Claus?"

Sean's father eyes him warily.

"What do you mean?" he says.

What the hell, Sean tells himself. *Might as well, now that you've started it—*

"I mean football, Dad."

"What about it?"

He isn't going to make this easy.

"Dad, we went to four different guys."

"Yeah?"

"They all said the same thing."

"They did not."

"They all said it would be risky for me to play football."

"It's risky to cross the street," says his father. "But are you going to spend all your life on the block where you were born?"

"It's not the same thing, Dad."

"Sure it is."

"This is my leg, Dad. That I walk on. That I stand on. My leg."

"Damrosh didn't think it was risky."

"Damrosh!" says Sean, dismissing the man as well as his opinion with a wave of his hand.

Damrosh had been the fourth and last doctor they'd consulted, the one his father had been looking for all along, the football fan.

"All he said was, if it happened again, he could probably fix it," says Sean. "Because he can work miracles."

"He's the best," says his father. "Roberts even said so."

Roberts was one of the other three doctors they consulted, one of the three that worried about the consequences of a second dislocation.

"Right," says Sean. "Thanks to Damrosh, there are guys playing football in the NFL today who all the experts had written off as hopeless cripples."

"That's right," says his father. "Higgins! LaRocca! Who else did he say?"

"Dad."

"Did he do Cunningham or was it Dorsen?"

"Dad," says Sean. "It doesn't matter. I don't want to be in a position where all the experts are writing me off as a hopeless cripple."

His father looks at him.

"Even if Damrosh *can* work miracles," Sean tells him, "I don't want to need a miracle to make it possible for me to bend down and tie my shoe."

He doesn't get it!

"It's over, Dad. I've decided."

Say it!

"I'm not playing any more football."

There!

His father blinks his eyes in disbelief.

"You have to!" he says.

Calmly.

Like there's no question about it.

Like it's Sean's duty.

"Why?" Sean asks him.

"Why?" asks his father.

He's getting angry now. The shock of what Sean's told him is wearing off and he's getting angry.

"Because!" he says, fighting to control his temper. "Because of all the time you've put in. Because of all the work you've done. Because of all the goals you've set for yourself!"

"What goals, Dad?"

"To be the best!" says his father.

"That's what it's about?" asks Sean.

"Yes," says his father. "That's what it's about. Being the best damned quarterback in the whole damned world."

"Being a winner," says Sean.

"In whatever you set out to do," says his father.

"No matter what it costs," says Sean.

"You pay the price," says his father.

"To get the winner's share of the glory," says Sean.

"Yes," says his father. "Is there something wrong with that?"

"No," says Sean. "I guess not."

"You *guess* not?"

"Except those aren't my goals."

"Since when?" asks his father.

"Since forever, Dad," says Sean. "Those are your goals."

"The hell they are!" his father shouts. "They're everybody's goals! Only not everybody has the stuff to achieve them. And you do. If you've got the guts to accept a little risk!"

Sean doesn't believe it!

"Jesus, Dad!"

"Everything in life's a risk," his father tells him. "Airplanes fall out of the sky. Soda pop bottles explode. Lunatics tamper with aspirin."

But Sean isn't listening. He didn't expect this to be easy. But he never thought he'd hear his own father accusing him of lacking guts. He never thought he'd see his father practically daring him to risk crippling himself.

For what? he asks himself. *For a trophy? For whom?*

He wants to cry, but he doesn't. He gets to his feet and takes his crutches and hobbles over to the window and stands there, looking out.

After a while, he hears his father heave a sigh.

"What do *you* want to do?" he says. "What are *your* goals?"

"I don't know, Dad."

"Of course you don't."

Turning away from the window, Sean looks across the room at his father.

He's sitting on the sofa in the conversation area, watching the guacamole changing color, looking utterly defeated.

"But I must be good for something more than just playing football," says Sean. "Don't you think?"

"Sure," says his father. "But what?"

"I don't know," says Sean.

"Shit," says his father.

He slams his hand on the coffee table and gets to his feet.

"You want a drink?" he says.

"You mean a *drink?*"

"Yes."

"No," says Sean. "No thanks."

"I do," says his father. "Several."

As he turns and moves off to the bar on the other side of the room, Sean watches after him.

"I love you, Dad."

"I know," says his father. "I love you, too."

"I know," says Sean.

Thirty-one

She was watching a tear, poised on the edge of her eyelid. She was waiting for it to spill over and inch down her cheek.

She was standing in her bedroom, looking in the full-length mirror that was mounted on the back of her closet door.

For the last fifteen minutes, she'd been trying on the clothes that her parents bought her for Christmas, slipping into slacks and skirts a full size smaller than she usually wore.

She'd been thinking what a pleasure it was, having such great parents, getting such nice gifts and being so slim.

It had occurred to her that she might make a fortune writing *The Heartbreak Diet Book*.

In the darkness, as she lifted her new raspberry cashmere sweater up and over her head, she'd laughed at the idea.

Between the weight she'd lost dieting for Buckley, and the weight she'd lost mourning him, she'd dropped over fifteen pounds in the last month.

But as she pulled free of the sweater and emerged into the light, she'd gotten a good look at herself in the mirror.

Standing there, with her jutting ribs and her hollowed cheeks and her sunken eyes, she looked anything but funny.

In fact, she was so much the picture of heartbreak, she'd been moved to tears.

It was humiliating.

Anybody could have told her that Buckley was a clown. People would have stood in line to tell her. But that wouldn't have stopped her.

Not Julie Stillwell. Once she'd made her mind up, nothing could have stopped her from throwing herself at Buckley, body and soul.

It wasn't just that she'd gone to bed with him. She'd never been that proud of being a virgin anyway.

It wasn't the lovemaking she felt cheated out of anyway. It was the love.

Buckley had made her believe he loved her, when all he really loved was himself.

He'd played her for a fool and a fool was what she was.

Looking in the mirror, she made herself a promise—it would never happen again.

Julie Stillwell would never let another boy fool her into thinking he loved her, and more importantly, she'd never fool herself into thinking she loved another boy.

She'd *had* her love affair.

And that was that.

Maybe, one day, she thought, when she was much older, she'd meet someone mature enough to appreciate her for her inner qualities.

Of course, by then, her outer qualities would probably be all wrinkled and saggy. But he wouldn't care.

Until then—until Mr. Old came along—she'd . . .

What would she do?

She'd pack her bag and get ready to drive into New York City with her father, tomorrow morning. That's what she'd do.

She tore herself away from the mirror and got her suitcase out of the closet. She opened it up on her bed and began filling it.

She was going to New York to baby-sit her twelve-year-old cousin, Catlyn.

Catlyn's mother and father, Julie's Uncle Larry and Aunt Linda, were flying off to the Caribbean for the week.

Their housekeeper, who usually stayed with Catlyn when her parents were away, had been promised a trip home to Jamaica to visit with her family.

So Julie's Aunt Linda had called and asked Julie's mother if Julie would be interested in spending the week in New York.

Julie's mother thought it was a great idea.

She knew Julie liked Catlyn and she knew that she loved New York.

And she thought a week of living in a Fifth Avenue apartment and mingling with the holiday crowds that thronged the city's streets might be just the thing to snap Julie out of her funk and get her back on her feet.

The only problem, she thought, was New Year's Eve.

She thought Julie might have made plans.

But when she asked Julie how she'd feel about spending New Year's in New York, Julie surprised her by saying, "Sure. Why not?"

Julie had been dreading New Year's Eve, ever since her friend Eleanor called and invited her to her party.

At first, Julie thought she might say yes to her invitation.

She didn't have a date, but being at a party, even without a date, would probably be a lot better than staying home and "celebrating" New Year's alone.

But then she got this picture of herself at Eleanor's party.

At the stroke of midnight, she saw herself standing all alone, waiting for some charitable stranger to come along and give her a kiss.

The way she pictured herself, she looked so pathetic, it was more than she could bear.

She told Eleanor she was sorry, but she'd already made other plans.

She'd also been invited to a party at Vicki Hanson's.

She thought it was great of Vicki to call and nice of her to say that she didn't want to lose Julie's friendship, just because their "mutual acquaintance" had "traded down to an inferior model."

But when Vicki admitted that she'd also invited their "mutual acquaintance" to her party and that he'd probably be coming with his "Swedish meatball," that did it.

It was bad enough watching Buckley every day after school, rushing to the parking lot and racing off to pick up his "Swedish meatball."

She didn't need to be at the same party with him, watching him nibbling on his hors d'oeuvres.

She especially didn't need to see him sneaking up the stairs with her and showing her the way to Vicki's little room in the attic.

She told Vicki she was sorry, but she'd already made other plans.

So tomorrow Julie was going to New York City, where she and Catlyn would probably welcome in the New Year with a hug and toast each other with glasses of grape juice.

But what the heck! If going to New York wouldn't do much for her, at least it would cheer up her mother.

Julie knew she'd been a horrible drag on her mother ever since the night of Buckley's opening, when she'd kept her up half the night, carrying on like a delirious three-year-old.

Her mother had been very sweet that night and for days after. She comforted Julie when she needed comforting and left her alone when she needed to be left alone.

And there wasn't a trace of pity in her sympathy. And there was no indifference in her detachment. And she didn't offer any advice until Julie asked her for it.

And then, when Julie finally asked her for advice, her mother told her about all the times she'd had her heart broken, and how, over the years, she'd discovered that the only sure cure for a broken heart was falling in love again.

Which didn't help.

Because Julie knew she'd never fall in love again.

But still, through all her moping and her baleful silences and her endless staring off into space and her sudden fits of sobbing, Julie's mother had done her best to be there for her.

But she wasn't a saint. Her patience was wearing thin, and Julie couldn't really blame her.

Her patience with herself was wearing thin, too.

She wished she could just say good riddance to bad rubbish or something equally wise and get on with what was left of her life.

But as much as she wanted to, she couldn't.

For now, the best she could do was to give her mother a break and get out from under her feet for a while.

She was trying to decide whether she should pack her new raspberry cashmere or not when the phone rang.

Without thinking, she walked over to her desk and picked it up.

"Hello."

"Hi, Julie."

"Who is this?"

"How soon they forget."

"Buckley?"

"In person."

"No, thank you."

She slammed down the phone.

The bastard! she thought.

The nerve of him! Calling up and acting like he wasn't the worst piece of—

The phone rang again.

Julie took a deep breath, gritted her teeth, and lifted the receiver.

"You're not the only one with a broken heart," said Buckley.

Julie said nothing.

"You may find this hard to believe, but I happen to love you, Julie. I mean it. But I also happen to love Kristin.

"I know that's supposed to be impossible," he said, "to love two people at the same time. But it isn't. Because I do. I love you and I love Kristin, too."

Still Julie said nothing.

"Kristin doesn't understand, either," he said. "But I told her I didn't care. I told her, just because I was seeing her, didn't mean I didn't want to see you anymore.

"I want to see you, Julie," he said. "I have to."

Still Julie said nothing.

"Kristin said I had to make a choice," said Buckley. "A choice between you and her. By the time she got back from Mexico. After New Year's.

"So I thought," he said, "if you weren't busy tonight, we could—"

"Go to hell!" she screamed.

And she slammed down the phone and burst into tears and threw herself onto her bed.

After a moment, the phone rang again.

At the top of her voice, Julie shouted, "I'm not here!"

Downstairs, someone answered the phone.

Upstairs, Julie sobbed into her pillow until she heard footsteps coming up the stairs, walking to her door.

"Julie?"

It was her father.

"Tell him to go fuck himself!" she shouted to him.

"Julie!"

"I mean it!" she shouted. "Tell him to—"

"Okay!" said her father. "Okay. I'll get rid of him."

Burying her head back in her pillow, she heard her father leave the room and plod back down the stairs.

Sometime later, not too long after her father had gone, Julie heard her mother climbing the stairs.

She felt like such a rat for putting her through this.

"I'm sorry, Mom."

Her mother walked over to the bed and sat down beside her.

Very quietly but very firmly, she said, "You've got to stop this now, Julie."

"How *can* I?" Julie cried.

"You have to make yourself," her mother told her. "Even if it means putting on an act."

"For *him?*"

"No," she said. "For you. You have to act like you're over him and keep at it, until you start to believe it."

"I'll *never* believe it."

"You have to start *now*, Julie!" said her mother. "Right now. Before you dig a hole for yourself that's too deep to get out of. Do you hear me?"

"Yes."

"Will you do what I'm asking you? Starting now?"

"I'll *try*," said Julie. "But tomorrow, okay? Okay?"

"Okay," said her mother.

"I told him," said Julie's father.

He must have been standing in the doorway. Julie couldn't look.

"Thank you," she said.

"I think I shocked him," said her father.

"I wish you'd electrocuted him!" said Julie.

Her mother laughed.

"That's the stuff," she said.

Thirty-two

Bzzzz . . .

April Addams opens her door.

"Hey! I thought we weren't getting dressed!" says Sean.

"Just a little something I threw on," April tells him.

She's wearing a black velvet and crepe off-the-shoulder evening gown. Her hair is cut very short and shaped like an English schoolboy's. Her big brown eyes are lined with violet. Her mouth is plum red.

She looks terrific—like a shy little girl and a sexy older woman, both at once, and all rolled up in one.

Until she opened the door, Sean considered himself pretty dressed up in his leather boots and his pleated slacks and Eurocut sport coat, but now he's feeling somewhere between informal and come-as-you-are.

But April doesn't seem to notice or care.

She kisses his cheek and takes his coat and looks at the cane he's leaning on and says, "Do you need that?"

"I don't know," Sean tells her. "Are you going to behave?"

She laughs.

"Scout's honor," she says.

"Okay," says Sean.

He hands her his cane.

She deposits it in a well-stocked umbrella stand near the door and leads him into her richly furnished living room, with its Persian rugs and fine antique furniture, its collection of fine paintings and its giant-size television screen.

The TV is on and tuned in to a big New Year's party that's being held in the ballroom of some big hotel somewhere.

Like the Stardust Room, he thinks.

On the screen, a bunch of well-dressed older people are jostling each other around a dance floor to the music of an old-fashioned dance band.

Like me and Sara Beth at the Stardust Room.

"Champagne?" asks April.

"What?" says Sean.

He wonders where Sara Beth is right now and why he is where he is.

"Champagne?"

"Oh," he says. "Yeah. Sure. Want me to open it?"

"It's open," says April. "You sit."

Sean sits.

April goes over to this little antique liquor stand and bar, lifts a bottle of champagne out of a polished brass ice bucket, and fills a long-stemmed glass with champagne.

Then, after refilling her own glass, she carries the two glasses across the room, hands one to Sean, and raises the other.

"To better times," she says.

"Better times," says Sean.

They clink and drink.

And then April joins Sean on the sofa.

They have about an hour to kill before midnight, but it goes pretty quickly.

April has to hear all about Sean's knee, about the injury and the consultations and the surgery and the physical therapy—all of it.

She's a big *St. Elsewhere* fan and she can't get enough of the gory details.

"So that's it," she says, when Sean's finally brought her up to date. "No more football."

"That's it," says Sean.

"It must feel strange, huh?" says April. "I mean, haven't you always played football?"

Sean nods.

"Since I was bigger than the ball, my mother always says."

"So?" says April.

Sean looks at her.

"What's it feel like, you mean? Knowing I can't keep on doing what I've always done?"

"I think I know," says April. "It's scary, huh?"

Sean nods.

"I used to bitch about playing ball," he says. "To myself, but—"

He shrugs and shakes his head.

"I liked some of it," he says. "The feeling you get when everybody's clicking together. There's nothing like it. And the attention. I liked that, too. And the girls. And the scholarships."

He laughs and waves to the air.

"So long!"

"But you used to bitch about it," April reminds him.

"Yes," says Sean. "I never liked playing as much as my father liked having me play."

"So whatever I did out there, no matter what it was, I was really playing for him. Or for the coach. Or for some scout with a scholarship to offer me. I wasn't really playing for me, you know? It wasn't ever my game. But it was the game I played."

"And now..."

He shrugs.

"I don't even know what the game is," he says. "Is there a game?"

"Sure," says April. "There's millions of them. You know that."

"Yeah," says Sean. "I guess."

"You just have to scrounge around until you hit on one that turns you on."

"I've been thinking about getting into film," Sean tells her.

He looks to see her reaction.

She doesn't laugh or even crack a smile.

"Maybe go to film school," he says.

"That's great," says April.

"I don't know," says Sean. "I'm just thinking about it. I've always liked photography and movies, so maybe . . ."

"I guess you'll be a director, huh?"

Sean laughs.

"Why do you think that?" he asks April.

He has no idea what he might be or even what there is to be. He's seen all those credits at the ends of movies, listing grips and best boys and assistant producers and production assistants and he doesn't have the vaguest notion what any of them actually do.

"Because the director's the one in charge," she says. "And that's what you're good at."

He smiles and shakes his head.

"It's not like football," he says.

"I thought everything was like everything else," she says.

"Maybe," he says.

"So who is she?"

"Huh?"

"Who is she?"

"Who is who?"

"The girl who's made you so sad," says April.

"Oh," says Sean. "You mean it shows?"

"I don't think I ever saw you sad before."

"Well." He shrugs. "It's New Year's, you know."

"Not for two and a half minutes," says April. "So? Are you going to tell me who she is?"

240

"Who she *was*," Sean corrects her. "I don't know who she was. I might have just made her up."

"Just to fall in love with," says April.

"Yeah!" says Sean.

That's exactly it!

He'd needed to fall in love with somebody and Sara Beth had made it easy.

"How did you know that?" he asks.

April shrugs.

"I do it all the time myself," she says. "It's one of the reasons I'm having my head examined."

"Because you make up people to fall in love with?"

"Yeah," she says. "And because these guys I fell in love with, even if I *did* make them up, I didn't make up how I felt when they said 'Thanks a lot, April, I'll see you around' or 'I'll call you.' And then they never did.

"Or maybe they did, once or twice. But then they stopped.

"That really *happened*," she says.

"I'm sorry," Sean tells her.

On the TV, they've switched to Times Square. You can see the big ball in the background, getting ready to begin its descent.

"It's getting close," says Sean.

Any second now, the countdown to the New Year will begin.

"I was afraid," says April. "I was afraid I'd get so scared of having my heart broken, I wouldn't have the courage to fall in love anymore. And if I thought I'd never fall in love again . . ."

She shrugs.

"What would be the sense of living?" she asks.

"There are other reasons for living," says Sean. "Besides being in love."

"Are there?" asks April.

"There'd better be," says Sean.

"TEN . . ."

The crowd in Times Square starts the countdown.

"NINE . . ."

"Are you crying?" asks April.

"EIGHT . . ."

"I guess," says Sean.

"SEVEN . . ."

April puts her hand on his.

"Go ahead," she says.

"SIX . . ."

"It's embarrassing," says Sean.

"FIVE . . ."

"I'm flattered," says April.

"FOUR . . ."

"THREE . . ."

"TWO . . ."

"ONE . . ."

"HAPPY NEW YEAR!"

"Happy New Year, Sean."

"Happy New Year, April."

She leans to him and kisses him.

It's a very gentle, very sweet kiss, more friendly than passionate, but deeper than friendly, too.

When it's over and April leans back away from him, Sean sees that she is crying, too.

But then she laughs and says, "It's catching."

Sean laughs, too.

"Do you think you could just hold me?" she asks.

"I think so," says Sean.

She comes into his arms and he holds her.

He holds her for all that he's worth until it's time for him to go.

And then, taking leave of April with a hug, he finds his way out of her apartment building and down to the street.

He walks until dawn.

He doesn't walk well and he doesn't walk without pain, but he walks.

He walks from April's house on Central Park West, all the way down to Greenwich Village and then back, through Washington Square and up Fifth Avenue.

After about four A.M., the city is strangely peaceful and he takes some of its quiet and its calm into himself.

He'd dreaded New Year's Eve, but it's turned out to be a good night after all.

April couldn't have been sweeter or more understanding.

She's a really terrific person and he's grateful he has her as a friend.

Sara Beth . . .

In a way, it's too bad about her.

Too bad *for* her, really.

Maybe things wouldn't have worked out between her and him.

Maybe she never intended them to.

Maybe Jack is the right guy for her.

Maybe she knew that all along.

Maybe she made me *up!*

It doesn't matter now.

He loves Sara Beth.

He always will.

He wishes her well.

And for himself . . . ?

There was never anyone before Sara Beth and there probably won't be anyone after her.

That's a bitter pill to swallow. But there's no point kidding himself about it.

It's possible, Sean supposes, that somewhere down the line, when his memories of Sara Beth have faded, he might fall in love again.

But it will never be the same.

Nothing will ever be the same.

Still, he knows it's possible to make a rich and meaningful life for yourself without having a woman you love to share your life with you.

You can devote your life to your work and your hobbies and your friends.

And you can find comfort and pleasure with women who you'll never love completely, in the way that you know you can.

Lots of people do it.

Maybe most people.

Some do it well.

Some do it badly.

He'll do it well.

Starting today, he'll pull himself together.

Who can tell?

Maybe with time, he might even wind up happy.

Stranger things have happened.

It's a new year. The old year is behind him. The world is alive with unexplored possibilities.

He hears music. The oom-pah of an organ.

He looks at his watch.

It's just nine A.M.

He's standing at the corner of Fifth Avenue and Fiftieth Street. The music is coming from the west.

Rockefeller Center, he thinks. *The skating rink.*

He wonders who might be skating at this hour.

He decides he'll take a look.

Thirty-three

"Happy New Year," said Catlyn.

"Says you," said Julie.

Julie had promised Catlyn she'd take her skating this morning, but when Catlyn woke her at seven A.M. and said, "Let's go," she'd forgotten all about it.

She sent Catlyn to phone Rockefeller Center and find out when the skating rink opened and then she went back to sleep.

But since the skating rink wasn't open at seven o'clock, there was nobody at the rink to answer the phone and tell Catlyn when it *did* open.

So Catlyn woke Julie again.

This time, Julie sent her off to call the nearest police precinct and find out if they knew when the rink opened.

They knew.

Catlyn woke Julie to tell her the rink didn't open until nine o'clock.

Julie thanked her for the information.

"I'm hungry," said Catlyn. "Aren't you?"

"Good morning," said Julie.

Although she had her doubts.

But now, as she sailed across the rink at the heart of Rockefeller Center, Julie was thinking Catlyn might be right.

Maybe the new year would be a happy one.

She'd been happy before without Buckley. Why shouldn't she be happy again without Buckley?

As a matter of fact, she wasn't so far from happy right now.

With everybody in New York City fast asleep or nursing a morning-after hangover, she and Catlyn had the whole rink practically to themselves.

The only people on the ice with them were this very old couple. Dressed in matching skating outfits, they were moving slowly and gracefully around the edge of the rink, taking turns supporting each other in an elegant dance routine that they must have been practicing all their lives.

Aside from them, there was only a guy sitting at the side of the rink, hunched over on a chair and lacing up his skates.

Tagging along behind Julie, Catlyn was a pretty steady skater and, with hardly anyone around, she didn't need much supervision.

It began to snow.

Julie tilted her head back and felt the gently falling snowflakes stinging her face.

Looking straight up the rose-tinted walls of the sky-scrapers that surrounded her, she saw a circle of creamy blue sky and imagined herself looking down a magical wishing well.

Closing her eyes, she wished herself a Happy New Year and then—*bang!*—she crashed into something and—*oof!*—she was flat on her back, lying on the ice, looking up into the face of this incredibly good-looking, terribly embarrassed, and unmistakably amused young guy.

"Sorry," he said. "I didn't see you. Are you okay?"

He had sandy hair and blue-green eyes.

"Can I give you a hand?" he said.

He reached his hand down to her.

She took his hand and then, acting on a sudden impulse, she yanked it—"Hey!" he shouted—and pulled him down to the ice.

He didn't move.

He just lay there, flat on his back, beside her, looking straight up at the sky.

For a second, Julie was afraid she'd hurt him.

But then he started to laugh, chuckling at first, but building up, louder and louder, until she thought he might laugh his head off.

Finally, when he got himself under control, he looked over at Julie.

There were tears in the corners of his blue-green eyes, but there was also this huge grin on his face, as he held his hand out to Julie and said, "Hi. Sean Manning."

Shaking his hand, Julie smiled and said, "Julie Stillwell. Nice bumping into you."

Which set him off laughing again.

"I guess I needed someone to knock me on my ass," he said.

"My pleasure," said Julie.

He looked over at her and smiled and kept looking at her.

"I guess I did, too," said Julie.

"Are you okay?"

It was Catlyn.

She'd skated over to Julie's side.

Without taking his eyes off Julie's, Sean told Catlyn, "We're fine."

Without taking her eyes off Sean's, Julie said, "Catlyn, this is an old friend of mine, Sean Manning."

As Sean smiled, Catlyn said, "Hi."

Still looking in Julie's eyes, Sean said, "Nice to meet you."

"You, too," said Catlyn.

She turned and skated away.

A moment passed.

"Well," said Sean, "I guess there's only one way to go from here."

He rolled over onto his stomach and got to his feet and reached both hands down to Julie.

She took his hands and, this time, she didn't yank him down to the ice.

This time, she let him pull her up, and as she came to her feet, she let her momentum carry her straight into his arms.

BRUCE AND CAROLE HART began writing for television in the late 1960s. They wrote some of the first scripts and songs for "Sesame Street" and also helped put together the Marlo Thomas special, "Free To Be . . . You and Me." They produced, directed, and—with Stephen Lawrence—wrote the songs for the television-movie "Sooner or Later," which was also their first novel. They also created and produced NBC's Emmy-winning series, "Hot Hero Sandwich."

The Harts write for young adults because they feel that "very few authors, filmmakers, television producers, etc., communicate honestly with young people about the important issues in their lives. Too often, this leaves young people feeling isolated, nonexistent, unimportant. It leaves them without a realistic perspective for dealing with their problems. We write to tell them that they are not alone and that what they care about matters very much—to them and to all of us."